Murphy

Book Five of
The Siblings O'Rifcan Series

By Katharine E. Hamilton

ISBN-13: 978-0-578-48458-7

Murphy

www.katharinehamilton.com

Cover Design by Kerry Prater.

This is a work of fiction. Names, characters, places, and incidents are either the product of the author's imagination or are used factiously, and any resemblance to actual persons, living or dead, business establishments, events or locales is entirely coincidental.

Thank you to all my readers who've followed the O'Rifcan family from book one until now. I love this family, and I'm so glad you guys do as well! Thank you for the support.

Acknowledgments

It's easy to write about a loving family when you have one of your own... thank you to all of my family members for their love and support.

My editor, Lauren Hanson. We've been together for eleven books now. No better person to trust with my voice as a writer.

Thank you to all who've shared their expertise with me for this series. Ninny and Papaw, L.K. Moerbe, Sherrill Crisp, and various others who've taught me the ins and outs of their trades. I appreciate all of you and your work.

And special thanks to my readers. We've had a whirlwind of a year and I can't thank you enough for embracing the O'Rifcan family. I've loved sharing them with you.

« CHAPTER ONE »

Whistling, his arms burdened with a load of empty crates, Murphy O'Rifcan strolled his way up the footpath from his mother's bed and breakfast and towards his pub on the corner. The stone building held charm in its rough exterior and warm interior; the appealing flower pots out front that his sister tended to for him, and the welcoming warmth that seeped out of its currently open windows. He could faintly hear the music he'd left playing. He nodded to a couple of locals on his way, greeted them with a smile and never stopped whistling. He was the jolly sort. Always had been. His mam had called him a child of the sun, because he brightened everyone's day, and he did his best to live up to that expectation. He gazed through the windows of his sisters' shop and paused, his tune still carrying as he squinted to peer through the large window. His lips twitched, his tune faltering as he flashed a quick grin. Setting his crates down, he opened the door and walked inside.

"And what have we here?" He held his hands out to his sides in surprise at seeing his youngest sister, Chloe, sitting at a long work table tying together flower stems. A florist, Chloe's latest project included bouquets for bridal portraits. Their brother, Claron, had found the love of his life in the form of American Rhea Connors, and the two lovebirds were on a fast track to matrimony. Chloe, however, was not meant to be on a track at all at the moment, her broken leg resting on a cushion in a chair in front of her under the table.

"Conor has me all fixed up." She grinned and motioned to the large brace wrapped around her leg.

"I can see that." Murphy walked forward and sat briefly on a stool nearest the table. "And how you be feeling, little one?"

"I've been better." Chloe sighed, but her hands never stopped working as she grinned up at him. "But it feels nice to be productive once again."

"I hope you aren't planning to do this all day," Murphy warned.

"That would be a no. Conor has me on strict orders. I am to do what needs to be done for Rhea's portraits and then he is going to see me back to my flat."

"Good. Handy having our Conor around."

"Indeed. Especially since he has to carry me up the stairs to me own home."

"Ah. Something tells me he doesn't mind." Murphy winked at her and she flushed. The newest romance to weave its way into the O'Rifcan family was between their childhood friend, Conor McCarthy, and his youngest sister. Their love for one another blossoming rather quickly, but not surprisingly to the rest of the family. It pleased Murphy to see his siblings so happy. Claron with his beautiful Rhea. Riley with his bombshell Heidi. Layla with her serious Delaney. And now, his littlest sister, his fairy, Chloe, and their friend Conor. All seemed to rapidly happen one after another. An epidemic. One he'd somehow managed to dodge, and gratefully so.

"Well, I will leave you to it then. I've got me own work ahead of me today. Prepping the pub for the evening rush. If your fella comes back soon, tell him I need to have a word. We've a stag party to keep planning. And if you find yourself in need of company this evening, give me a ring. I'll fetch you."

"Thanks, brother." Chloe turned up her face and he kissed her lightly on the cheek.

"Don't work too hard, little bird."

"Promise." Chloe flashed one last smile as he stepped back outside and retrieved his crates. He saw Conor making his way up the footpath and decided to wait to grab a quick minute with his friend.

"And there be the man of the day." Conor beamed as he slapped a friendly hand to Murphy's shoulder. "Visiting my beauty, I see."

"Aye. Making sure you've given her proper care," Murphy teased.

Conor laughed as he rubbed a hand over the back of his neck. "What she'll let me give, I am. There be that O'Rifcan stubbornness that's been giving me a few fits."

Murphy laughed. "Oh aye, I imagine so."

"So what's the craic?"

"Clary's stag party. Have you and Riley come to definitive terms? Declan and I have some thoughts."

"Riley be making his way here this evening from Limerick for the family meal. Perhaps we can all think on it then?"

"Sounds like a plan," Murphy agreed. "I should have a moment's respite. Piper be coming from Galway to help me this evening."

"Slowly winning her over, eh?"

"Slowly... possibly. She be the stubborn one these days."

Conor laughed. "I have faith in you, Murphy. Keep at her."

"I intend to."

Conor reached for the doorknob to Chloe's shop. "Be seeing you."

"Aye. G'day." Murphy picked up his crates and his tune once more, a personal rendition of 'Kiss Me I'm Irish' that carried his feet to a new rhythm allowing him to meander his way at a slower pace towards his pub.

The door was ajar which brought his whistling to a sudden stop as he lightly nudged it open, his eyes adjusting to the darker interior. He smelled her before he saw her. The familiar scent of vanilla and strawberry, like a cupcake. Piper's blonde head popped up from behind the counter and he startled. She grinned. "About time you showed up, O'Rifcan."

∞

Piper O'Beirne grinned as the look of annoyance replaced the brief concern on Murphy's face. She was early for her shift at the pub, but she hadn't expected to give him a scare. She swiped the bar with a polishing cloth. "And where've you been off to this morning? Neglecting your chores?"

"Chores?" Murphy held up the crates in his hands. "Fetchin' some crates. A *chore.*"

"Ah, and were those crates at yer mammy's place? Did you get a hot breakfast? A nice cuppa?" she teased, her hands on her hips.

"And what if I did?" Murphy challenged with a smirk. "Me mammy loves me, no reason to deny her the chance to showcase her love for her favorite child."

"Favorite, are we now?" Piper's brows rose as she shook a finger at him. "Careful with those words, there's too many of you O'Rifcans. One of your siblings might overhear and call your bluff."

Murphy laughed. "'Tis true." He set the crates in the back room and fetched two boxes of beer. Nestling them into the ice tubs behind the bar he looked up. "And what brings you here so early from Galway? Finally come to your senses and decide to work here full time?"

"Don't count yourself so lucky just yet, Murphy O'Rifcan." Piper sighed as she went about the room and wiped down chairs. Sensing his watchful gaze, she turned her back to him and squatted to wipe the base of one of the tables. She didn't want him to see that his comment, as flippant as it was delivered, actually hit the nail on the head. No, she hadn't quit her job in Galway yet. But the more Murphy continued to ask and the more her work and life in Galway grew stagnant, the more her temptation to drop everything and move to Castlebrook increased.

She reminded herself of how hard she'd worked over the years to make a name for herself. She managed a pub on Cross Street, one of the busiest and most successful pubs in Galway, and yet lately, the city felt stifling. She'd been helping Murphy for over six months and every trip to Castlebrook was full of fun, family, and fresh air, three things she did not have in the city.

"Earth to Piper?" Murphy's voice broke through her thoughts and had her back straightening. "Everything okay?"

"Fine." Her answer a bit too quick, his brows rose.

"Are you sure? You seem a bit distracted."

"Just thinking."

"Care to elaborate?"

She smirked. "Careful love, your nosiness is showing."

He rubbed the tip of his nose for effect and had her laughing.

"Just a lot on me mind."

"Fella problems?" Murphy leaned his elbows on the bar and peered down at her, wriggling his eyebrows.

"No fella, no problems." She shrugged.

"That's a shame. I figured that was the only competition I had left in Galway."

"No. Your only competition is me, myself, and I."

"Ah, and they are proving to be quite difficult." Murphy admitted. "Well, you know the offer is there. I'm not going to keep bashing you over the head with it. I am going to Limerick this weekend to check out a lad there. Riley says he's quite good."

"Limerick? Riley?" Piper felt a small stab of betrayal. Not that the position at Murphy's was hers and she didn't want someone else taking it, but Riley. He's the one that scouted her out. His allegiance was to her. *Allegiance*? She inwardly rolled her eyes at herself. Murphy had every right to look elsewhere because she had yet to accept the position. If anything, she figured he was just baiting her so that she would commit. But Murphy O'Rifcan was not prone to lying, and the fact that he didn't continue to bait her with this other man's credentials rang the bell of truth at his words as well. Piper now had more competition than herself. Murphy needed help. If she didn't take the position at his pub, he'd find someone else. She wasn't sure how she felt about that. Yet, she was also impressed to see the business-minded Murphy appear. His request for her help usually seemed half-hearted and appeared as though he'd wait until she finally acquiesced. But now, he was actively in pursuit to fill the position. Disappointment settled in her chest. She wasn't quite sure she was ready to take the plunge to Castlebrook, but now, it seemed, there was a time clock on the decision.

∞

When Murphy walked into the familiar two-story cottage, the family home, he spotted a set of suitcases by the stairwell. After all her children had flown the nest, his mam decided to open their home to visitors. Sidna's Bed and Breakfast had guests floating in and out on a regular basis, after all his mam ran a tight ship. But he was surprised to see the man standing next to the bags. Paul Connors. Rhea's father. Murphy smiled. "Couldn't keep you away, I see." He extended his hand and Paul shook it heartily.

"Came as soon as my shift was over. Retirement has been a blissful eleven hours thus far." He laughed as Jeanie, Rhea's mother, walked down the steps and beamed at the sight of Murphy. It was no secret the woman held a soft spot for him, and the feeling was mutual.

"Hi there, sweetie." She hugged Murphy and then reached for one of Paul's bags while Paul grabbed the other. "Did you see my surprise?" She looked at her husband in adoration and Paul lightly tapped her chin.

"I did. A right good looking one at that." Murphy winked at her as she grinned.

"Everyone is in the kitchen hounding your poor mother."

"Ah... must have just removed the bread. I smell it, and that tends to have us all losing our heads."

"I believe you're right. I'm going to get Paul settled and then we'll be back down."

Murphy nodded and listened as Rhea's mother excitedly began filling Paul in on all the wedding details that had come to fruition. He smiled at their backs as the front door opened and the man of their conversation stepped inside shedding his boots at the door. Claron.

"Well, if it isn't me little brother," Murphy greeted with a nod. "Was just visiting with your future in-laws."

"Paul made it in?" Claron asked.

"Aye. Just now, I believe."

"Good. Rhea will be happy about that."

"And where is our dear Rhea? Coming in from Limerick tonight?"

"Afraid not." A frown marred his brother's brow and Murphy gave him an encouraging pat on the shoulder. "

"Won't be long and she'll be here all the time. Then you'll be wanting her to make trips to Limerick just for some peace."

Claron eyed Murphy as if he'd grown an extra head. "I could never grow tired of Rhea," he defended.

Murphy chuckled. "I don't say it to be mean, brother. 'Tis normal for two married people to want some space every now and then. Just ask Da. Why do you think he and Roland escape on their fishing trips every now and then?"

"Escape?" Still offended, Claron just shook his head. "I hate being separated from Rhea. When she's not here, I feel like a part of me is missing. I can't think of a day when I would want that feeling willingly."

"Always the romantic." Murphy winked at him as he made his way to the kitchen, Claron on his heels. The room was boisterous, active, and brewing with life. Just as it always had been. The comforts of such a room directed by his mam who even now was barking orders at his oldest sister, Lorena, to fetch the glasses for the table.

"And you, boyo," She pointed to Riley who had just stepped into the room via the back door and hadn't even set his keys down. "Wash yer hands and then set the utensils." Riley stood with outstretched arms as if his arrival warranted much more than a chore, but he quickly did Mam's bidding. Her sight fell upon Murphy and she pointed to the wine bottles on the side counter that had yet to be opened. He obeyed, winding the cork screw into the first bottle, a resounding pop encouraging his sister, Layla, to swoop next to him and steal the bottle from his hand. She filled a glass and began to sip.

"Can't wait until supper?" Murphy asked her.

"It's been a dreadfully long day."

"Has it now?" He eyed her again as she took a long gulp of the stout wine making his own throat burn just watching her. "Will Delaney be joining us?"

Her eyes flashed and he immediately knew why it had been a dreadful day.

"No," She said. "Apparently his work is more important right now. Can't seem to pull himself away."

"And that bothers you?" Murphy asked, curious as to how his sister was just noticing Delaney's workaholic tendencies.

"No. Yes. A little. Just today."

"And why today of all days?" Murphy asked.

"Because 'tis our two-month marker. We should be celebrating. Toasting champagne, eating a romantic meal, and—"

He held up his hand to stop her and she grinned wickedly before pouting once more.

"I imagine our Mr. Hawkins will make it up to you, Layla Aideen. He'd be a right fool not to." Murphy tapped her nose before she released a contented sigh, the effects of her wine chugging starting to sink in.

"I know you're right. 'Tis just hard not having me way."

Murphy laughed at her honesty. Layla had always been quite spoiled when it came to men. She'd had her fair share of relationships and flings, but she was always the one in control. But since Delaney Hawkins stepped into the picture, Murphy could only respect the man for the way he handled his sister's wild spirit. Miraculously, Delaney seemed to warrant a new side of Layla that no one had ever seen. And more, Layla liked him because of it. She playfully patted Murphy's shoulder as she held out her glass and he topped it off before she wound her way towards the dining room.

"Clary, love. Fetch yer in-laws, won't you?" Sidna called. "Or give a shout." She pointed to the back stairwell that nestled in the corner of the kitchen. "Supper's hot and about to be on the table."

Claron didn't have to make a sound as Jeanie and Paul entered through the main kitchen entrance with full smiles. Jeanie immediately began to help carrying dishes to the large table as the back door swung open and Claron Senior stepped inside, followed by Roland, Rhea's grandfather. The two men were inseparable and elusive, especially when it came to pre-dinner prep. Surprisingly, they were tailed by his brother, Tommy, whose crestfallen face did not go unnoticed by their mother. Sidna marched towards her son and grabbed his arm, pulling him towards the island where she continued slicing the bread loaves. They spoke in hushed tones and Tommy's nervous habit, just like Riley's, was to rub the back of his neck with his hand. The poor fella looked miserable. Murphy walked towards him with a glass of wine, and Tommy looked up appreciatively as he sidestepped his mother and began talking to Murphy.

"'Tis Denise troubles."

Murphy's brows rose. He didn't say a word. He didn't have to. 'Twas a gift being who and what he was, such that people felt they could share their burdens with him. An open ear. An unbiased opinion. And a decent pint normally. People traveled to his pub to vent or celebrate, and he was there. His brothers needed a listening ear, and he was there. It was his natural position in the order of things, and it was no surprise that Tommy continued spouting off about how Denise wished to take a break for a while. Heartbroken, but trying to maintain his bravado, Tommy just shook his head in disappointment.

Murphy slapped him on the shoulder. "Cheer up, lad. It couldn't come at a better time."

"Oh, and why's that?" Tommy asked, doubtful.

"Because we have Clary's stag party this weekend, and you won't have to worry about the woman nagging you."

Quick to defend, Tommy eyed his brother in annoyance. "Denise doesn't nag."

"Ah, well then, at least you won't have to worry about making the nightly phone call for sweet dream wishes whilst we are all having fun."

Tommy just shook his head and walked off. Shrugging, Murphy made his way towards the dining room carrying two bottles. He set about filling glasses and beamed when he saw Chloe already seated in her spot, Conor beside her.

"Aren't you two sneaky," he pointed out.

"Aye." Chloe fidgeted, trying to find a comfortable position for her leg under the table. "Best to sit early than navigate with this beast." She pointed to Conor instead of her leg and had them all laughing. Conor playfully tugged one of her red curls as Murphy went about his way. He sat across from them, their love and warmth too contagious to pass up, as everyone else began filling in other spots.

Claron Senior held up his glass. "Welcome to our new guest." He looked towards Paul. "And soon to be family. We can't wait to have your Rhea as an O'Rifcan. To Rhea and Clary."

"To Rhea and Clary," everyone repeated.

Jeanie swiped a quick tear from her eye and realized it hadn't gone unnoticed by Murphy. He winked at her before receiving a slap on the back of his head from Riley who'd sat beside him. Jeanie chuckled as Riley flashed her a dazzling smile.

"Boys." Senior's voice boomed down the table at them and they immediately gave up their shenanigans in favor of passing the food around.

"How's your Heidi, brother? Working late hours like Rhea and Delaney?" Murphy asked.

Riley nodded. "Aye. Though I plan to kidnap her in a bit, take a long stroll about Limerick before bedtime."

"Awfully late for a walk, love." Sidna tsked her tongue. "Best let her rest and then treat her to a wonderful meal tomorrow."

Riley's brow rose at his mother's response. "I think I will keep me plans, Mam, but thanks."

"The poor dear is probably exhausted. Clary spoke to Rhea earlier and she sounded like a wet fairy."

"You didn't speak to her, Mam," Claron interjected.

"Aye, but I could all but hear the poor dear," Sidna continued, making everyone bite back smiles at her infamous earwigging.

"Now, Sidna," Senior began.

"Don't 'now, Sidna,' me." She swatted his hand as she looked to Riley once more. "Those young women be workin' hard so they can take off early on Friday for Rhea's gathering in Galway. Delaney be doing the same so he can attend Clary's stag party. Leave them be, or better yet, let them rest."

Riley turned to his plate, ignoring his mother's request. Murphy knew Riley would still be making the drive into downtown Limerick to see Heidi. The woman had bewitched him from the start. However, the feeling was mutual, and Murphy knew that after a long day, Riley's presence might be exactly what Heidi would need.

"And is Piper manning the kegs at the moment?" Sidna asked, looking to Murphy.

"Aye. She is."

"You'll take her a warm plate when you're done," she ordered, turning back to her conversation with Lorena.

"She's got her boss hat on tonight, doesn't she?" Claron whispered.

"A bit more so than usual," Murphy admitted, noticing how tired his youngest brother looked. "You hanging in there, Clary?"

"Aye. Just busy as of late."

"Tends to happen when you're preparing for the rest of your life."

Claron chuckled. "Aye. 'Twill be worth it in the end."

"Of course it will," Murphy assured him. "Best save some energy for this weekend though. We boys have grand plans."

"I imagine you do." Claron grinned as he forked a mouthful of the freshly snapped green beans that his mother had blanched to perfection.

"I wonder what the women have planned? With Heidi and Layla at the helm, one can only imagine." Murphy's grin widened at the thought and Claron just shook his head at his brother. Murphy nudged him. "Come on, Clary. Aren't you just a wee bit curious?"

"Curious? Maybe, but I've plenty to think on right now besides Rhea's weekend with the lasses."

"You hope it's just with lasses," Murphy murmured and then cringed when Claron's green eyes grew sharp. "Kidding, brother. Only kidding."

"I'll have you know," Chloe interjected. "That we intend to shop, eat expensive meals, drink only the best champagne, and shower Rhea with love and lingerie all this weekend. No crazy shenanigans for us." She looked to Claron and smiled, hoping to ease any concerns he may have from Murphy's influence.

Murphy wriggled his eyebrows, "Now that is a pretty picture."

Claron looked to him again and Murphy choked back on his words.

"I think it best if you just stop talking, brother." Chloe giggled as Claron's face finally broke into a grin at Murphy's discomfort.

Murphy nodded. "Aye. Don't want me hole growing any bigger."

"Wise." Claron smirked as he continued to eat, casting an amused glance towards Chloe.

«CHAPTER TWO»

Greedy hands tapped on the bar as Piper hurried her way from one patron to the next, filling pint after pint. She glanced up at the clock above the bar and inwardly scolded Murphy for not returning at the time he'd said he would.

"Lass!" The obnoxious man of the evening hollered from the opposite end of the bar, his slurry speech and sloppy hand gestures a sure sign he'd had more than she served him. "Another, lass!" he called.

She slid a pint to an awaiting hand in front of her and then walked towards the man, swiping down the bar top as she went. "Another pint," the man gurgled as he resituated himself on the stool and almost slipped off.

"I think you should sit this next pint out, lad." Piper flashed a charming smile as she fixed him a tonic water on the rocks. "Refresh yourself for the pretty lasses that will be filtering in for the music."

Insulted and not falling for her flattery, the man spit on the floor as his cheeks turned red. "I asked for another pint."

"And I said you've had enough. Best calm yerself, or I'll have to ask you to leave." Her tone was calm, not wanting to cause a scene or ruffle his feathers any further, but the man wasn't having it. Spittle clung to his beard as he stumbled to his feet and rested the majority of his weight against the counter. He was a tall man, and though she was of the shorter sort, he still outstood several of the taller men she'd seen for the night. He had a robust chest, a shirt with various stains, and he reeked of cigarette smoke. Though Murphy did not allow smoking inside the bar, she could smell the man's habit clinging to his clothes.

"Where be Murphy?" The man pounded his fist against the bar. "I will have a word with him." He shook his finger at her. "And you best hope he doesn't fire ye."

Piper's lips twitched of their own volition, only making the man angrier. He grabbed his glass of tonic and tossed it at her, the liquid contents splashing against her face. Several people gasped and waited to see what Piper's next move would be.

She was used to intoxicated patrons. She hadn't worked in a pub for over ten years and not encountered her fair share. Memories of her father's worst moments filtered through her mind at the moment as well, but she'd never had a drink tossed on her. That was a first. And it made her blood boil. She reached across the bar and grabbed the man's ear, pulling him to within an inch of her face. His yelps for help went unnoticed by the other amused patrons. Piper hopped the counter and swung her legs over, her grip never loosening as she pulled him towards the entrance. "Teach you to toss a drink at me," she told him. "You should be ashamed of yerself," she chided as she opened the door and flung him outside. "Best be getting home now, and I don't want to see your face in this pub for at least a week."

Baffled, the man held a hand to his ear as he hurriedly patted his pockets for his car keys. Piper jingled them in the air. "No driving for you tonight," she continued. "Get to stepping."

The man turned and pulled up straight when he bumped into a surprised Murphy. He then grabbed Murphy's lapels and began blubbering about his mistreatment. Murphy tried to pull back from the stale breath and sweaty fingers, but the man held strong. He gave a friendly pat to the man's shoulders. "Best listen to our Piper, Seamus. She only has yer best interest at heart."

"My keys. She took my keys," the man whined.

"And I shall return them to you on the morrow," Murphy assured him. "On ye go now." He nudged the man further up the footpath and watched as he zigzagged his way towards home, which Murphy knew wasn't that far. He then turned to see a wet Piper standing before him.

"That his doing, then?"

"Aye. Tossed his drink all over me. The bloody eejit."

Murphy pulled out his cell phone.

"What're you doin'? You're a half hour past the time you said you would return. Now yer makin' calls?" Exasperated, Piper turned to walk back into the bar until she heard Murphy's conversation.

"Aye... Seamus. Assaulted Piper. I think he needs a night to think on it. Thanks, brother." He hung up.

"What did you do?" Piper asked.

"Gave Declan a call. He's going to pick up Seamus, give him a night in a cell to think over his actions."

Her face went void of color. "Murphy, no. The man just needs to sleep it off. I don't want him getting into further trouble, even if I am madder than a hornet. I'm not the type for layin' boots."

"Aye. I know you're not. But Seamus should know better than to treat you that way." Murphy walked towards the door and opened it. His eyes widened at the rowdiness before him. Two men leaned over the bar top and helped themselves to fresh bottles while another crew baited one of their friends to top off their pints.

Piper stood behind him, stunned. Murphy raised his fingers to his lips and let out a shrill and powerful whistle that caused everyone to freeze. The music played on, but all eyes were on Murphy. "We're closed!" He yelled. "Out! All of you!" he motioned over his shoulder to the door. "Fetch the handheld, will you Piper?"

She hurried and ducked under the bar and grabbed the small key pad. She handed it to Murphy at the door. He closed out tabs as people exited, accepted the loose cash from those willing to tip after being kicked out, and when the last person left, he shut the door with a slam. "Bloody Martha!"

Piper began collecting glasses as he ducked under the bar door. "'Tis there a full moon tonight?"

"No idea," she admitted, her head bowed as she tried to think of a way to apologize for letting his pub get so out of control. The truth was, she had never had such an issue before in Galway. Never had an entire pub full of people lost their marbles.

"Here." He took the few glasses out of her hands and set them on the counter. "Take this." He handed her a warm plastic container. "Eat."

"What?" Confused, she looked down at what he'd handed her.

"Are you hungry?" He asked, dipping his head so as to look into her eyes for the truth.

"Truth? I could eat a reverend mother."

Murphy chuckled. "Then eat. Me mam wouldn't have it any other way. I'll collect glasses for now."

"But—" Perplexed, she watched as he went about his work.

"But what?" he asked, looking up.

"But aren't you mad?"

"Why would I be mad? Seems to me everyone else has lost their bloody minds."

"But I was to man the bar tonight. 'Twas on me to watch things... and they went hairy."

"And I don't believe a collection of fools is yer fault."

Relieved and appreciative, Piper slid onto a stool. "Thanks, Murphy."

"For what?" He rested his hands on his hips as if he had no clue as to why she'd be thanking him.

"For being understanding."

"When people decide to run me pub to their own devices, they don't deserve to stay. And customers will *not* be tossin' drinks on me employees. That is automatically going to get them thrown out."

He heard a tap on the door and saw several customers waiting to come to the pub for a night of fun. He walked towards it and unlocked it. Pretty females dressed to break hearts batted their lashes at him. "Sorry ladies, the pub is closed for the night."

A series of high-pitched disappointments could be heard as well as several flirtatious flatteries towards Murphy. In his usual friendly demeanor, Murphy suggested a pub in Limerick for them to take their charms for the night. He shut the door and locked it once more.

"A shame to turn away customers." Piper forked a bite of the stewed meat and closed her eyes. His mammy could cook, and she thanked the stars she'd be staying at the B&B for the next few days. Murphy watched as she shoveled the food and ate like a teenage boy. His brow lightly lifted. "What?" she asked around a mouthful.

He smirked. "Nothing. Just curious as to how a little thing like you can put food away like Conor McCarthy."

She tossed a towel at him and he laughed. Self-conscious now, she took a smaller bite.

"You attending Rhea's gathering this weekend?" he asked.

"I planned on it. Unless you need me here?"

"No, that's alright. I'll be closing the pub on Friday evening until Saturday evening."

"I work Saturday in Galway. Off Sunday if you need me to man the kegs while you party with the lads."

"I imagine they'll be wrapping up by then, but thanks."

"Any grand plans for Clary's stag weekend?" she asked.

Murphy leaned across the counter and popped a green bean from her plate into his mouth. "And why would I be telling you our secrets?"

She rolled her eyes as he laughed. "Very well then. Guess I'll keep our plans a secret as well."

"Chloe said you ladies will be shopping and showering Rhea with gifts."

"All true," Piper finished, her tone indicating there was more to the story.

"But—" Murphy prodded.

Piper shrugged with a sly smirk. "I'll leave the rest to your imagination."

Laughing, he grabbed the crate of dirty glasses. "Now, that's just torture. But it will have to do for now." He held up the crate. "I'll be tendin' these if you'll reset the bar when you're done."

Nodding, she watched him walk through the swinging door into the back room. If what had just happened occurred at the pub in Galway, she would have been fired on the spot. Again, she found herself contemplating Murphy's offer about working for him full time.

Her cell phone dinged with an incoming message and it was her boss in Galway. Her pay raise was just approved. Sighing, she set the phone aside. And that was one of the reasons it would be hard to leave Galway.

∞

"Just cinch it up, lad! Tighter!" Declan yelled across Angel's Gap, hoping Riley would hear him. He unclipped the walkie talkie from his pant pocket and waved it in the air hoping one of his brother's would at least pick up the device on the opposite side.

"This be yer captain speaking." Murphy's voice drifted over the walkie and Declan rolled his eyes.

"What the devil's he doin'?" Declan barked.

"It would seem our architect brother is finding faults in your design plan, Dec."

Growling in frustration, Declan looked to Jaron next to him. "Why can't he just bloody trust me?"

Jaron smirked and crossed his arms as he leaned lazily against the tree behind Claron's house. "Maybe it's because the last time you designed something, Riley broke his ankle... in three places."

"I was thirteen," Declan reminded him.

Jaron shrugged. "And that matters?" He laughed. "At least we will all know it's safe once Riley gives it a once over."

"No fun, the lot of ye." Declan bit back a grin as he held up the walkie to his lips. "And what's the verdict, brother?"

Static came through the line before Murphy's voice. "He is now cinching the cable around the tree. I repeat, around the tree. One clamp is closed." A pause. "The second clamp is now closed. I repeat, we are down to only one clamp left."

Riley's mutter of "Eejit" towards Murphy could be heard over the walkie.

"Third clamp complete," Murphy reported.

Declan sighed. "Finally. No wonder his projects take forever to complete."

Jaron harrumphed as he stepped forward to see if his brother needed additional help on the next step. "Conor should be here any minute. Took the pipe to drill holes for me," Declan told him.

"Pipe?" Jaron asked.

"For the handle."

Jaron nodded. "Think Clary will even do this?"

"Why wouldn't he?" Declan asked.

"Because it's bloody dangerous would be my guess," Jaron retorted.

"That's the point. A wee bit of danger is good for a man every now and then. Especially Clary."

"Hm. Right." Jaron's sarcastic reply had Declan turning.

"You don't think he'll like it?"

"I think you will. And Riley. And Murphy. Possibly Jace."

"But you don't?"

"That would be a definite no." Jaron chuckled at his brother's disappointed face. "Let's just say I would like to see Conor McCarthy fly across the river before I test its strength."

"Speaking of." Declan's handsome face split into a pleased smile as their friend hurried towards them carrying a plastic pipe in his hand. "Conor, that was fast."

"Aye. Not too difficult to drill holes."

"Not too difficult to put a bloody cable around a tree, but yet that still took Riley forever," Declan grumbled. He surveyed Conor's craftsmanship. "'Tis perfect." He fetched a thick cord and began threading it through.

"Are we to trust your knots?" Jaron asked.

Declan smiled. "Of course." He looked up at his brother and deviously wiggled his eyebrows. "I don't plan on losing one of you just yet." He tightened the first knot. "These are just reinforcement. There be a screw that goes here and will bolt to the trolley."

Jaron and Conor exchanged a brief look of concern. "You going to test it first?" Jaron asked Declan.

"I will if it stops yer nagging and eases Riley's mind."

"Um, Murphy here." Murphy's voice cackled over the walkie. "Riley is a wonderin', well, I guess we both are... how do you plan for us to send you the cable to attach on your end?"

Declan walked over to a cardboard box and fetched his son's remote-controlled helicopter. He began flying it across the Gap towards Murphy. He heard his brother laugh as Riley just shook his head.

"Thought of everything, he has," Conor guffawed as he watched Riley tie the end of the cable to the helicopter and Declan began its journey across the river. The weight of the cable stretching altered his flight pattern, but the small copter rested on the grass and Jaron began untying the cable.

Declan wrapped the cable around the tree, threading it through a plastic hose to protect the bark, and then began clamping it. The zip line was now complete. He reached into the box that housed the helicopter and pulled out a small sling.

"What's that?" Jaron asked.

"For those who wish to sit while they zip instead of hold on for dear life. That way no one falls in the river to their untimely death."

"You think it would kill us?" Conor leaned over the edge of the cliff to survey the River Shannon below.

Declan shrugged. "No idea, but I'd rather not take the chance."

"We should ask Clary. He'd know how deep it is down there," Jaron suggested.

"Aye. Possibly."

"Where be our Clary?" Conor asked.

"Milking," Declan reported. "I wanted to get this set up while he was busy, so it'd be a surprise."

"Thought Buddy was to be taking over the farm while Clary's busy this weekend."

"After the last milking. Clary said after that he was free."

"Are we testing this or what?" Murphy's voice fluttered over the walkie and he and Riley stood on the opposite side with hands on hips, waiting.

Declan clipped the sling to the trolley and pulled it over his head. "Here goes nothing."

"If you die, Aine will kill us," Jaron told him. Declan's amused smirk was the last thing they saw as he pushed off the side of the cliff and zipped over the line towards Riley and Murphy.

Murphy cheered and all the men had smiles as wide as the Gap as Declan reached the other side in one piece and with obvious excitement over his success. Murphy hurried and fit himself in the sling.

"I can't wait."

Riley rolled his eyes. "He was wanting to be the first attempt," he explained to Declan.

"I'm glad one of you is excited. Jaron's been nagging from the beginning." He shoved Murphy off the cliff and his brother hooted and screamed as he flew across the river to the other side. When he landed, he leaned back and let out a primal scream towards the sky that had everyone laughing.

"Exhilarating!" Murphy beamed as he slipped out of the sling. "Remind me to invite Declan to every party I have."

He offered the trolley to the other two men. Jaron took a cautious step back. "No thanks."

"Ah, well... can't damper the lad's excitement." Conor took hold of the handle and Murphy helped him into the sling. "A wee bit snug."

Murphy chuckled as he helped give Conor a push off the cliff. He watched as their friend's bright red hair zoomed across the landscape, Conor's natural grace causing him to barrel into an awaiting Declan. Jaron and Murphy laughed.

Riley walked towards his truck on the other side and Conor hopped in. Declan zoomed back across the river towards Claron's house. When he landed, he unhooked the trolley from the cable. "All set."

"Nice work, brother." Murphy slapped him on the back. "'Twill be a fun night and weekend with that, for certain." Riley and Conor pulled to a stop in front of the cottage and exited Riley's truck.

A horn honked and Layla's red sports car pulled in in beside them. "What's she doing here? I thought they'd already be in Galway?" Declan asked.

Layla hopped out of the car as the passenger door swung open and the sight of Chloe struggling to pull herself up out of the vehicle had Conor running towards her. The obvious joy on both their faces gave Murphy a brief pound to the heart to see his little sister so loved.

"And what have we here?" Layla pointed to the zip line.

"None of yer concern, sister," Murphy told her, his hands on his hips. "This be man country now. On with ye." He waved towards her car.

She laughed. "Easy, brother. I'm only here because Rhea wished to leave Clary a gift for this weekend." She extended a bright blue gift bag. "Make sure he gets it, won't you?"

Murphy took the bag and nodded.

"That's a lad." She patted his shoulder. "Now, I just have to pull Chloe away from Conor and we'll be on our way and you fellas can get back to whatever death trap you wish."

Riley stepped out of the cottage already sipping a beer. "Delaney coming still?"

"As far as I know," she answered. "I'm sure he forced himself at least a half day's work before thinking of fun. I was hoping to catch him before I left."

Riley shrugged. "Send me any pictures of Heidi this weekend... you know... if you think I need to see them." He winked.

"Gross, brother. I will not be sending you sexy pictures of your girlfriend. Besides, I imagine Heidi will be doing that all on her own."

"That she will." Riley grinned and had Murphy chuckling at the disgust on Layla's face.

"Make sure Piper has a good time, won't you?"

Layla's right brow rose. "And that be a concern for you, why?"

He shoved his free hand into his pant pocket and shifted on his feet. "She had a rough week. She deserves a bit of fun."

"Hm." Layla considered his request. Still suspicious of his reasoning, she shrugged. "I'll do me best."

Another car pulled up the drive and Layla squealed as she darted towards it. Delaney had barely stepped out of the vehicle when Layla jumped into his arms. They slammed back against his door as she assaulted him with passionate kisses.

Riley gave a low whistle. "Her way of staking her claim before she leaves. Giving him something to think about."

Murphy laughed and watched as Layla pulled back and a disheveled Delaney cupped her face and gave her one last peck on the lips before walking hand in hand towards the brothers.

"Del," Riley greeted, handing him a beer.

"And where's the man of the hour... or weekend, I should say?"

"With his girls. As always." Murphy pointed towards the barn as they saw the last rotation of cows enter inside.

"Did any of you think to help him?" Layla asked. "So he would finish quicker."

Their blank expressions had her rolling her eyes. "Of course not."

"We've been busy," Riley defended.

"Aye, I see that. Setting up your death trap." Layla shook her head in mock dismay as she waved towards Chloe. "Come, sister. Let us leave these fools to their adventures. We have our own to see to."

Conor pulled Chloe's hand to his lips. "Be careful. If you need me, just call," he told her.

"I'll be fine." Chloe gave him one last long kiss. "Have fun. Relax. And don't die."

His typical jolly laugh had her grinning as she crutched her way towards her sister's car. When the women had left, the barn door opened and Claron began his walk up the hill followed faithfully by Rugby, his Irish Setter, and Holstein, his cat.

«CHAPTER THREE»

Piper stood dumbfounded as she stared up at the luxurious townhome before her. She'd found her feet immobile as soon as the address came into view. Clearly, Rhea's Aunt Grace possessed great wealth. Though Piper assumed, the confirmation of it was seen in the woman's deluxe accommodations. She never quite knew how to act in such surroundings. She'd met Grace before, loved the woman, but she had no idea this is where the woman came from. How was she to relax in such a house? How were they to have a rowdy bachelorette weekend in such a pristine and expensive place?

"Gawking, are we?"

Layla's voice had her jolting in surprise.

Piper cleared her throat. "Just making sure I have the right place."

"This is it," Chloe confirmed. The youngest O'Rifcan still a bit bruised up from her car accident, struggled to shift her crutches over the small pebbled walkway. "Don't be intimidated."

"I'm not," Piper lied.

"You'd be the first." Chloe chuckled. "First time I came to Grace's I felt me stomach tie up in knots I felt so out of my element. But 'tis not bad once you're inside."

"I love coming to Grace's," Layla said as she pulled her and Chloe's suitcases from the back of her car.

"Of course, you do," Chloe replied on a laugh.

"She spoils us rotten," Layla assured Piper. "Come on, let's shower Rhea with fun."

The three of them stepped up to the door, the brass knocker in the shape of a lion further taxing Piper's nerves. She wasn't used to luxury. Growing up with a single dad and a crotchety grandmother had given her a lifestyle with minimal indulgences. Bare bones, simple meals, and second-hand wardrobes were the norm. Since living in Galway, she'd made it her mission to create a stable life for herself. A life where she could indulge every once in a while. But Grace's home was on an entirely different scale for Piper.

The door swung open and Heidi stood holding a silver tray with mimosas resting in champagne flutes. "Come in, ladies. Come in." She beckoned them inside. "You're just in time."

"In time for what?" Chloe asked.

Heidi pointed to the drinks. "We just whipped these up. Rhea's in the kitchen... Hurry, she's trying to be creative."

Piper's attention went to the black and white chessboard floors, the sweeping stairwell of rich mahogany with a wild leopard-print runner trailing down the whole of it. The walls were painted a pale and inviting pink, like the subtle tinge of a rose petal. The floor to ceiling windows in the entry lit up the entire front half of the home. The bold colored furniture, the charismatic art on the walls, and the scents of feminine perfume definitely captured the Grace she'd come to know. Not a trace of masculinity was found in the place unless you counted the scandalously clad figures in some of the paintings that graced the entry hall.

She followed the other women into a large and open kitchen. The island held twelve stools across the length of it; stools with cushions wrapped in the same leopard-print fabric as the stairs. A bit ostentatious, yet fun, the house now seemed the perfect place for a bachelorette weekend.

"And where be Grace?" Piper asked, as she took a satisfying sip of her mimosa.

"On a trip." Rhea smiled as she gave Chloe a small hug around the shoulders in greeting. "One of her 'suits' whisked her off to Barbados for the weekend."

Piper's brows rose but she did not comment as Heidi held up her glass for a toast. "To a fun weekend. To an amazing friend. And to a life full of happiness with our dear and sexy Claron."

Rhea giggled as she excitedly toasted her glass to the others. "Thank you all for showing up and celebrating with me." Her smile split her face, leaving a certain glow that could only come from pure happiness.

"You have two weeks, Rhea. Two weeks before you're Mrs. Claron O'Rifcan," Layla reminded her. "We best make them count."

Heidi set her glass down on the counter and clapped her hands. "And on that note, we should begin." She grabbed a piece of paper that held handwritten notes on it and cleared her throat.

"We have a game for you, Rhea. A game that requires your full participation. You must agree to the following terms before we begin."

"Oh no." Rhea sat on one of the stools. "I'm all of a sudden extremely nervous at what you guys have come up with." Her gaze flicked from one mischievous grin to the next.

"So," Heidi continued. "Rhea, do you solemnly swear to complete all tasks requested of you?"

"What sort of tasks?" Rhea asked.

Heidi held up her finger. "No, no, no... you have to commit or not commit. You do not get a sneak peek at what's in store."

"That hardly seems fair." Rhea chuckled. "But I will commit."

"You swear?"

Rolling her eyes, Rhea nodded. "I swear."

"Good." Heidi set the piece of paper down. "First stop for us today is dinner at a swanky place Aunt Grace reserved for us. After that, your first test— or quest, I should say— will commence."

The women scattered, each taking residency in one of the rooms to dress and ready themselves for a night out in the city. Piper chose a fitted cocktail dress in deep plum, the A-line fit giving the simple dress a bit of flare. She partnered the look with nude shoes, the heel so pointed and thin, she wondered if she were nuts for attempting such a feat. But when she eyed herself in the mirror, she liked what she saw. Her blonde hair was cropped closely around her chin, the silky strands behaving for once as they showcased her heart-shaped face and strong jaw. A stubborn jaw, her dad always said, and a sentiment echoed by Murphy as of late. She thought about Murphy and wondered what the boys had in store for Claron for his stag party. She knew Murphy had provided the drinks, as he always did for family functions, but he was tightlipped on what shenanigans the men had planned.

A knock sounded on her door and Chloe poked her head inside, her eyes brightening at the sight of Piper. "Look at you." She hobbled her way inside, her red curls pulled back with but a few tendrils hanging to frame her face. She wore an iridescent halter with fitted black jeans, her leg brace blending into the color. Her sandals were bedazzled to match her top. "I think you're the stunner," Piper told her and Chloe laughed.

"Oh, aye, with me top that matches the bruises on me face. Such a stunner."

"Hey, it works."

Chloe grinned. "I wish I could wear insensible heels tonight. Instead, I'll be the short one... well, shorter one," she amended. She was petite as it was, but even tiny Piper now stood an inch or two taller than Chloe. She could only imagine the tall women hovering over her for the night. But in true O'Rifcan form, Chloe's dour demeanor did not last long and she beamed. "'Twill be nice to parade around a bit tonight. I haven't been out in quite some time."

"Aye, likewise."

A pounding resounded on the door. "Best hurry it up ladies, our chariot awaits," Heidi's brazen voice called through the door, her footsteps sounding on the marble on the other side.

"And off we go." Chloe opened the door and smoothly made her way out the door, followed by Piper.

Rhea descended the stairs in a dress the color of pearls, with a sweeping boatneck that showcased her beautiful shoulders. She wore her hair in a French twist, and simple diamond studs graced her ears. Around her neck she wore the rose necklace Riley had gifted her at the flower festival. She looked elegant and gorgeous and all the women smiled up at her as she hit the bottom step and stumbled. Layla caught her arm on a laugh. "There's our Rhea." Rhea playfully swatted her as they exited the house and a black limousine awaited them.

"I could get used to this type of transportation," Layla told them. She leaned her head against the cushioned headrest and sighed. "Though Delaney would think it a wasteful expense."

"As would most men," Piper pointed out.

"Riley's rented us a town car before," Heidi chimed in. "It was for this romantic dinner he planned for us. It was nice. But at the end of the night when you're wanting to—"

Rhea waved her hands. "Okay, we get it." She giggled at Heidi's unapologetic face. "You couldn't be as romantic as you'd like to have been."

"Exactly." Heidi beamed.

"I could see that being a problem," Layla considered, her mind wandering to Delaney and a dreamy look crossing her face.

Heidi shoved her arm. "No daydreaming about our men tonight."

Piper seconded the motion. "Those of us without one would prefer to feel included."

Chloe patted her leg as the other women grinned.

"Then perhaps we should find you one," Layla countered, her right brow slowly rising.

"No." Piper pointed at her. "This be Rhea's night. Not mine. And I'm perfectly fine without one. I have Murphy hounding me enough as it is, I don't need a boyfriend to do the same."

"Our Murphy." Chloe shook her head. "'Tis one of those men you can't help but love, yet he certainly has a way of almost irritating you out of it."

"All the time," Piper told her. "Just the other day he showed such kindness to me," she began, her voice turning almost as dreamy as Layla's had been. "He was so unaware of it as well. And then, bam... back to the real Murphy, annoying me about me job here in Galway and how I should leave it all behind for his pub."

Rhea chuckled. "It's a credit to your work ethic, Piper. He sees value in you. That's a good thing, even if his pursuit might be a bit annoying at times."

"I guess you're right. The eejit."

The sisters laughed and nodded in agreement.

"No better friend than our Murphy," Chloe told her.

"And no better nuisance," Layla added.

"Sounds like the perfect combination." Heidi slid towards the small bar against the side window and began pulling out a bottle of champagne. "We might as well." She popped the cork and Layla hooted in celebration as she passed glasses around.

"To Rhea." All the women toasted as they sipped and watched the city lights pass by. When they reached their destination— a five-star restaurant along the River Corrib— the driver opened the door and extended his hand to help each one of them to their feet. As they waited for Chloe to balance herself, Heid adjusted the top of her dress, causing every man in attendance to melt into puddles. Piper wondered if the gorgeous Texan even knew the effect she had on complete strangers. As she bypassed the line towards the podium at the entry, Heidi draped her arm around the squirrely man behind it and held a hand to her lips. "Ladies and gentlemen, the future Mrs. Claron O'Rifcan!" She motioned towards an embarrassed Rhea as the line clapped an offered congratulations. Pleased with the outpouring of love, Heidi then whispered to the man that they had a reservation. He handed them off to an awaiting attendant and ushered them inside.

"Did she really have to yell?" Rhea whispered to Piper on a laugh.

Piper placed a hand at the small of Rhea's back as they walked and leaned in to respond. "I don't think subtlety is in Heidi's vocabulary."

"That is true," Rhea reminded herself as she accepted the seat at the head of the elegantly set table.

"Compliments of Grace." The waiter held out a bottle of champagne that had Piper's eyes widening. The other women, witnessing her reaction, assumed it was an expensive treat. He began to pour and then several attendants began placing appetizers and hors d'oeuvres on the table. Clearly Grace had prepped the restaurant for their arrival.

Though Piper worked at a nice bar and had visited some of the nicest places in Galway, this was on a scale way out of her pay grade and she felt somewhat uncomfortable. She honestly could go for some of Sidna's cooking and be content, and by the way Chloe nudged what looked like escargot around her plate, she thought she might feel the same way.

A jingle fluttered through the air and Heidi slipped her hand into her clutch for her phone. "Hey there, handsome. I thought we agreed not to call one another this weekend."

She held the phone to Rhea. "It would seem you have a phone call."

Rhea grinned as she accepted the phone. "Riley, to what do I owe the pleasure?"

"Hi there, love." Claron's voice filtered through the line and her face brightened into that glowing grin once again. "Claron. Hi." She covered her grin and her eyes sparkled in the candlelight as whatever Claron said to her had her holding back tears of joy.

"And I love you," she finished, handing the phone back to Heidi. Heidi held it up to her ear.

"Now don't be calling again, Claron. This is a girl's weekend," she reprimanded. "Oh, hi Riley. I was scolding your brother for his interruption and turning Rhea into mush. She's going to be completely hopeless for the next half hour."

The women chuckled as Rhea nodded in agreement with her statement. "Oh, well, I'm wearing a—"

Layla snatched the phone from her ear and hung up the call. "There'll be none of that, thank you."

Heidi shrugged as she retrieved her phone and slid it back into her purse.

Piper's phone dinged and she reached into her bag to check her text messages.

Murphy: *"Any snapshots or juicy tidbits you wish to send me of your girl time would be greatly appreciated."*

Piper: *"And why would I do that?"*

Murphy: *"It would seem all me brothers are completely at a loss without their women."*

Piper: *Really? That's cute. I don't think the women feel the same way."*

She took a quick snapshot of Layla chugging back her champagne like a shot and sent it to him.

Murphy: *"Burn."*

Piper chuckled and Chloe leaned over.

"And what has you giggling over here?"

Piper showed her their conversation and Chloe laughed. "Fun to see me brothers love sick. I wonder if Conor be miserable as well?"

"How could he not be?" Piper winked at her as she put her phone away in time for the main course to flood the table.

∞

So far they'd sat on Claron's back porch, drank beer, and talked about Riley's remodeling plans for the cottage. Meat was on the grill, crisps were being passed around, and Murphy was bored out of his mind. He eyed the text from Piper, disappointed that she hadn't continued to text him just so he could have something to do. Conor slapped him on the back and leaned over.

"We should take matters into our own hands." He whispered, a glint sparking in his eye.

"Think so?" Murphy asked.

"They be content sitting here all night if we let them."

"Looks like it."

"So?" Conor prodded. "I'll go first."

Murphy's lips twitched and he set his beer aside. "Race you."

Conor tore out of his chair and off the porch as Murphy followed, shoving him aside to fight his way forward. The other men watched in surprise until understanding dawned on their faces.

Declan beamed as he took off at a sprint as well.

Murphy reached the zipline first and pushed off the cliff before even having set himself in the sling. Sheer grit helped him hold on for his life as he flew across the river. When he landed on the other side, he screamed and beat his chest as if a primal need for showcasing his win had overtaken him. Conor laughed as he tried to gain his breath. The other men made their way towards the cliff while Murphy zipped back across, this time sitting in the sling.

"You lived." Claron slapped his back on a laugh. "Your grip that first go around looked a bit dicey."

"Saw me life flash before me eyes a couple times, for certain." Murphy grinned as he panted for breath. "Your turn, little brother."

Claron shook his head. "I'll pass this round. Conor be ready it seems."

Conor, snug in the sling, accepted the assistance of Jaron and Riley off the side of the cliff and soared across the river. Claron eyed the line closely and the clamps securing it to the tree.

"Already surveyed the construction, brother." Riley's eyes danced as if he could read Claron's thoughts. He leaned in close. "Now, don't disappoint yer brothers. They worked hard on this for you."

Claron walked towards the rest of the crew as Conor zipped back across the line. When he stepped out of the sling he looked towards Riley. "I think we should head around to the other side so as to keep a momentum going. No one there to catch me fall." He chuckled as he handed the sling to Claron. "On with ye now, Clary. Feel the wind beneath yer wings."

Claron slid the sling around himself and stepped towards the cliff drop off. Music blasted up his driveway and had them all turning, but Murphy shoved him in the middle of the back and off the cliff before he could change his mind.

A loud scream of "Bloody Murphy" could be heard as Claron zoomed to the other side.

Tommy and Jace walked up from the arriving vehicle and towards the commotion.

"What have we here?" Jace asked, his navy gaze roaming over the winded Claron on the other side.

"You have to come back, Clary!" Murphy yelled.

Claron shook his head as he held up a finger for him to have a moment to catch his breath.

"Clary did it, hm?" Tommy asked. "How did you manage that? He being scared of heights and all."

Murphy's eyes widened a bit before he looked to Riley and they both laughed. "I bloody forgot about that."

"Me too." Riley's lips flashed a sparkle before he composed himself. "He's not going to come back across."

"Probably not." Declan, hands on hips, waited patiently. "He looking a bit green over there?"

Conor hooted in laughter which made them all grin. He looked to Delaney. "You be venturing across next?"

Delaney, somewhat standing aside to observe the brotherly interaction, cleared his throat. "Perhaps in a bit."

"Best have a truck load headed to the other side so the line keeps moving." Murphy, echoing Conor's earlier suggestion pointed towards a hesitant Claron. "Just in case Clary doesn't get up the nerve—" He was silenced by the sounds of the pulley raking against the cable as Claron soared back towards them. When he landed on his feet, he quickly relieved himself of the sling and tossed it on the ground.

"And *that* is how it's done, brothers." Beaming, he swiped his hands together as if removing the filth of the day. "Tommy, Jace, glad you could come."

"If Mammy could see this, she'd have a heart attack," Jace laughed.

"Best she not then," Murphy tossed over his shoulder as he took another turn, his loud wail echoing through the Gap.

Jaron just shook his head. "Daredevil, that one." He slapped a proud hand on Claron's back. "Conquered yer fears and kept yer stomach. I'd say that's a good fly."

"Me stomach hasn't quite caught up, so I can't promise I won't lose it," Claron admitted.

"Lives on a cliff but can't handle heights." Riley tsked his tongue. "A walking conundrum." He looked to his brothers. "And why are you two so late?"

Jace's dimples peeked as he grinned. "I was having a last-minute dinner with a pretty lass." He tossed a thumb towards Tommy. "Picked this one up from Roland's."

"Ah. And how is our Roland?" Riley asked.

"Good. A new television. He needed help with the set up."

"I wonder why he didn't ask me to help him?" Claron asked.

"He knew you were busy with the milking and that it was your special weekend, brother. He didn't want to steal your time."

Murphy landed with a thud as he appeared back on their side of Angel's Gap. "No one was planning to drive to the other side, so I figured I might as well come back over. Come on, Delaney. Take a turn," he invited.

Claron began walking towards the back porch, the meat on the grill needing tended. The brothers, followed by Conor and a quick-moving and relieved Delaney, settled into the seats they'd previously vacated.

"And what says Rhea of this death trapeze?" Tommy pointed towards the zipline.

"She doesn't know about it," Declan explained. "None of the women do except the only two women who could not care less if we hurt our noggins. Chloe and Layla."

"And Layla's a secret keeper these days?" Jace asked on a laugh before catching the disappointed and warning glare from Delaney. He sobered but bit back a smile at the man's loyalty to his sister.

"Aye. Well, we hope so. Though Rhea knows Clary be in good hands," Declan continued.

"My hands," Murphy interrupted. "All's right in the world with Murphy O'Rifcan in charge."

"And who named you as the captain?"

Murphy grinned. "I did."

"I'm the oldest," Declan pointed out.

"Wrong. Lorena be the oldest."

"The oldest brother," Declan corrected. "And you know what I meant, eejit."

Murphy's eyes danced as he continued to bait Declan. He caught the fresh beer Declan tossed a bit too high and towards his face on a laugh as Claron eased against the porch railing.

"You getting nervous yet, Clary?" Jaron asked.

Claron shook his head. "Not in the slightest. More impatient than anything."

"Don't blame you there." Jace toasted towards Claron. "Rhea be a fine lass, indeed. I'd be ready to"—

"Easy, brother. That be Clary's future wife you be talkin' of." Tommy warned.

"Was going to say, I'd be ready to *marry*," Jace finished and then batted a sly wink towards Riley. "You're a lucky lad, that's for certain."

"Aye," Riley agreed. "Our Rhea will have a special place in me heart forever and for always. Something about her sweet spirit touched me from the start. I'm glad we be making her family."

"I'm glad you are all on board with the idea. Not like it would stop me any way." Claron grinned as he took a sip of his drink. "Not sure what she loves about me, but I'm glad she's found it enough to marry me."

"I was a bit surprised she didn't fall for Riley," Jace added and had all the brothers and friends staring at him in surprise. "What?" he asked. "He rescued her on the side of the road when she was most vulnerable. They've had a connection from the start. And Riley... well, even I have to admit his skills in wooing a lass are on an expert level. 'Tis a wonder Rhea didn't fall for it, is all."

"I didn't try to woo Rhea," Riley pointed out. "Nor did I want to."

"Liar," Jace challenged.

"Not lying. She be beautiful, that's a fact. And kind. But there was something different about her," Riley explained. "And then when I saw her interact with Clary, I knew. She was his. Fated it seemed."

Claron smiled in appreciation as Riley toasted towards him. "Besides," Riley continued. "My Heidi suits me more than fine." He held up his phone to reveal a picture Heidi had sent him earlier of herself all dressed up and ready to go out and about in the city. Her dress clung to her curvaceous body and her gorgeous smile held a touch of mischief, and Riley's eyes softened as he studied it once more before slipping his phone back into his pocket. "She's all I need and everything I want."

"When did she send you that picture, brother?" Murphy asked.

"Earlier. They be headed to dinner somewhere fancy."

"I'd love to see a snapshot of Rhea all dressed up," Claron told him.

"I don't have pictures of *all* the ladies," Riley told them. "Only mine. If you want pictures, then ask for them."

"I thought there was a 'no contact' rule?" Delaney asked already reaching for his phone. Tommy swatted it from his hand. Delaney, surprised by the action, stood shocked as the others laughed.

"If the lasses want to send pictures, they will," Tommy told them. "Otherwise, leave them be."

"He's just grumpy because his lass doesn't want to send him pictures," Jace mumbled.

"My lass has nothing to do with this because she's not in Galway with the others."

"Apparently she's not with you anymore either." Jace knew how to expertly weave his way under his brother's skin. He'd always possessed the gift, Murphy thought. If any of the brothers could start a fight, it was Jace. Most of the time he didn't mean his jabs or comments to be riotous, but Murphy sensed he was beggin' for a fight.

"Enough, brother. Stop rubbing your new romance in everyone's faces." Murphy attempted to lighten the mood. "I don't have a pretty lass sending me pictures and I don't want to feel left out, so let's think of something else to do."

Grateful for the change of topic, Tommy shot him a thankful nod.

Murphy clapped his hands. "Now, Clary, when do we eat?"

«CHAPTER FOUR»

They'd successfully packed away more food than was planned, but as they climbed into the limo, Piper settled next to Layla and nodded that she was ready for her part in the evening.

"Rhea love," Layla snapped her fingers to gather the other women's attention. "Piper has a word for you."

Rhea looked up expectantly.

"Since I will have to work a brief spell tomorrow at the pub…" Groans flooded through the limo in disappointment and Piper smiled. "I know, I know… but only a brief minute or two. Then I will join you all again. But," she continued. "Tonight, we are to stop by me pub for Rhea's *first* gift."

Rhea rubbed her hands together and then grew nervous. "Wait... what do I have to do to earn my gift?"

Layla rolled her eyes. "Not near enough, if you ask me, but Piper be kind."

Piper shook her head and winked at Heidi. "There's a marvelous treat that awaits you at me pub. And you must consume it all in order to earn yer gift."

"Consume?" Rhea's brows rose. "I just ate enough for ten people."

"Ah, but not dessert." Piper grinned as they pulled to a stop outside her pub. "Come." She led the way inside, waving at a few of her coworkers as she pointed to a round table in the far corner. A handsome man came and placed a glass in front of Rhea. "A Guinness float," Piper announced.

"Trust me, it's ridiculously delicious," Heidi said, as she reached for a spoon.

"Rhea, if you will." Piper pointed to the spoon by Rhea's hand and she dipped it into the chocolate ice cream. Taking a hesitant nibble, her eyes lifted in pleasure.

"I think I can manage this." She grinned as the other women grabbed their spoons and helped her along anyhow. When they'd polished off the float, the same man appeared and set a bright pink gift bag on the table. He hurried away back towards the bar. Piper slid the bag towards Rhea. "My gift to add a little dessert to yours and Clary's after-supper conversations." She winked as Rhea removed the tissue paper and reached inside the bag.

Rhea giggled as she pulled out a can of whipped cream, a bottle of chocolate syrup, and a pair of spiky high heels. Piper bounced her brows as Rhea covered her mouth with her hand and laughed.

"Now that is my kind of lingerie." Heidi took the can of whipped cream and gave it a little shake before Rhea snatched it from her hand. "And I'm impressed, Piper. I'll remember this when I get married."

Piper grinned. "I wanted to incorporate something Clary-oriented, but all I could think of was the dairy, which led me to thinking of cream. So there ye go now, Rhea." She winked as Rhea reached over and squeezed her hand in thanks, a light tinge of pink staining her cheeks.

"Thank you, Piper."

Heidi clapped her hands. "Now, we are off to the next stop." She began to shuffle out of her chair as the other women gathered their purses and did the same.

"Piper." A man's voice interrupted their exit. When Piper looked up, her boss was by her side. "Aiden." She smiled in welcome and waved a hand towards her friends. "Out with me lasses tonight. We treated our lovely bride-to-be to one of the Guinness floats."

He forced a polite smile as his eyes held trepidation. "Congratulations." He told Rhea before turning back towards Piper and gently taking her arm to lead her a few steps away.

"What is it?" Piper asked. "Something wrong?"

"He's here again."

Aiden could have tossed a bucket of ice water over her head and not have chilled her less than the words he'd just spoken. "How long?"

"About ten minutes. I tried to explain that you were off for the evening, but he saw you. I have him in the kitchens."

Regret had Piper's shoulders sagging.

"You said this would not happen again."

Not knowing how to respond, Piper received the scolding she knew she deserved. "I'll take care of him. Sorry, Aiden. He knows better."

Aiden just shook his head and rubbed a hand over his jaw. "He caused a bit of a scene when he entered. I was able to contain it for the most part, though he did insult some of our customers. It cannot happen again, Piper. I hate to say this, but... if it does, I'm going to have to let you go."

Her heart sank. "I understand. You have me word."

"Aye. That's what you said last time."

She felt Chloe tap her elbow. "Alright there now, Piper?"

Piper watched the other women walking towards the exit and looked to Chloe. "I may have to meet up with you ladies in a bit. A little emergency has come up."

"Everything okay?" Chloe asked, seeing the bewildered expression on Piper's boss's face.

Piper briefly pinched the bridge of her nose before offering a pleading look to Chloe. "Give Rhea my regrets, won't you?"

Chloe squeezed her shoulder. "Would you like me to stay with you?"

Piper shook her head. Though she was touched Chloe would offer not even knowing what she was volunteering for, Piper did not want the sister to miss out on the fun that was planned for Rhea or to meet her father. "No. Thanks. It's just me Da. He's a bit of a— well, let's just say he likes his drink and giving away his money. He's here at the pub and I need to take him home."

Sympathy flashed in Chloe's eyes as she nodded. "Text or call me when you're free. I'll report to you where we be."

"Thanks, Chloe."

Chloe offered another smile and a brief nod towards Aiden as she crutched her way to the car.

Piper turned back to Aiden and they walked towards the kitchen. Piper heard her father before she saw him, and his sloppy rendition of Wild Rover had the hairs on the back of her neck standing to attention. It was always the song he'd sing when he'd come in from a late night out on the lash. And usually he'd end up making a fool and a mess of himself. Her Nan, bless her, had always tried to protect Piper from seeing him in such a state, but she wasn't an idiot. Her father was an alcoholic. It didn't take a genius to figure it out, and even at the age of eight, she knew the signs. Now, she spent most of her time working as much as possible, not only to take care of herself but to pay any of her father's outstanding debts or bar tabs.

She wasn't enabling him, she reminded herself. She just didn't want to see him end up dead. And Nan— her wonderful Nan— had to deal with the man all day and night. The least Piper could do was help with the financial burden her father had become to the both of them.

"Aye, there she is. Me daughter. The liar," he slurred, as his portly figure bent too far forward and nearly toppled off the stool. "Said you were working this weekend and what have we here?" He tossed a hand over his shoulder towards the exit. "Out with friends. Dressed like yer worth a fortune. Well, we all know better, don't we?" He growled as she hefted him to his feet and began leading him to the exit. Aiden followed closely behind, and as they entered the dining area, her father yanked his arm from her grasp. "I can walk meself home. No need for you to play the role of loving daughter." Piper continued guiding him towards the door as his voice rose and customers began turning their direction. Aiden attempted to shield the customers' views, but to no avail.

"Piper O'Beirne, my one and only offspring, my only disappointment, my only hindrance to having a good life!" he yelled as she shoved him out the door.

As they stepped outside, Piper caught Aiden's disappointed gaze. "I'm sorry, Piper," he told her. "But I must think of what's best for the pub. I'll give you a glowing recommendation, but 'tis time you find a new place."

She nodded, though inside her heart ached. She'd worked so hard and yet, once again, her father ruined one of the few good things she had in her life. She escorted him a couple of blocks before calling for a cab, and when it arrived, she shoved him inside, paid the driver, and sent him home to Nan. She took a stabilizing breath and looked up at the evening sky, the brightness of the day slowly fading into cooler hues of blues and grays. The city was alive with music, laughter, and fun, but Piper felt herself slipping into sadness just like the sun slipping behind the horizon. Her eyes burned as tears threatened to burst forth, but she wouldn't let them. She wouldn't give her father the satisfaction. She took a shaky breath and heard her phone buzz in her purse. With trembling hands, she pulled it out and bit back another frustrated sob. Murphy. She couldn't talk to him right now, not when she'd just lost her job. He'd only push harder for her to join him at his pub. But the call continued to ring, and she couldn't *not* answer him either.

"Hello there, Murphy."

"Ah, Piper love," His voice was cheery and tinged with a bit of whiskey as he garbled some of his words. "I've a question for you."

"Alright."

"You know that case of Jameson? Where did we place that? Do ye remember, love?"

"Sounds to me like you don't really need it."

He chuckled. "It's not for me, thank you. 'Tis for the *future groom*." he emphasized. "And what's the story with you? You sound a wee bit off your normal mark."

"Nothing, I'm fine," she lied.

"You be with the girls? I don't hear them. I figured you lasses would be flying high on champagne and strawberries... or rainbows perhaps."

"Because that's what we do in our spare time, ride rainbows." Piper responded dryly, rolling her eyes, though a smile tugged at her lips. "I believe the Jameson is on the last row, top shelf in the store room."

"Ah. There's a lass. I knew you'd know."

She heard him cover up the receiver and order what sounded like Tommy to fetch the crate. "All's well then, Piper?" he asked again, his voice a bit more serious.

She bit her trembling lip before taking a deep breath. "Yes, Murphy. All is well." She could tell he didn't believe her, but for once, Murphy O'Rifcan held his tongue and didn't pry.

"Alright then. Guess I'll give you a farewell for now then. I'm to deliver the goods to the lads. We've been flying most of the day."

"Flying?" Piper asked.

"Aye. It's amazing. Clary even did it. Thought don't tell Rhea. She'd think we were trying to kill him."

Confused, Piper agreed. "Okaaaaaay. Well, have a care, Murphy."

"Aye. You too, lass. And thanks again." He hung up on a yell towards one of his brothers and she smiled softly down at her phone. Murphy never seemed to have a care in the world. Always cheerful and helpful. Always brightening the day of those around him. She wondered if he ever really did fall into bad moods or temper tantrums. As she texted Chloe to check for their location, she listened as the ripples of the River Corrib harmonized with the sounds of the city. She inhaled a deep breath, breathing in Galway. Breathing in the scents and sounds she loved. As she exhaled, she envisioned the breeze carrying those thoughts and memories towards a new direction and adventure. One she knew she'd be embarking on months ago, if she were honest with herself. A new life in Castlebrook.

∞

Murphy hoisted the crate of whiskey onto his shoulder as he and Tommy walked towards the cottage. His steps faltered when he heard voices coming from the direction of the barn. When he turned, he spotted his brothers all leaning against the fence, Riley sitting on the top rung. All faced towards Conor's property on the other side. Murphy whistled towards an aloof Tommy and nodded towards the opposite direction. Rerouting, Tommy shuffled down the hill towards the barn, moving quicker than Murphy due to not having to carry an extra load.

"And what has you all staring into nothingness? Is it fairies? Are they out again? Beauties, the lot of them," Murphy chimed as he walked forward and set the crate on the ground at his feet. Holstein, Claron's cat, wound his way along the edges, nuzzling his cheek against the wood of the crate before slowly arching his way towards Murphy's ankles, completing simple figure eights of pure adoration until Murphy bent down and ran a hand over the length of him. Satisfied, Holstein wandered off. Rugby, on the other hand, barked and ran through the tall grass on the other side of the fence. As Murphy stepped forward and rested his arms over the top rung, he spotted Claron and

Conor attempting to coax one of Claron's cows out of the field and through the gate towards the rest of the herd. The cow had no intentions of moving.

"Have you all had a go?" Murphy asked.

"Why would we?" Jace asked. "This is Clary's business. The cow whisperer."

"Some whisperin' he's doing now," Jaron joked as Claron kicked the ground in frustration and started yelling for the cow to move.

"He wouldn't even have to bother with this if we'd chosen somewhere else to have his stag party." Jace, annoyed with the bovine interruption, rolled his eyes on a sigh.

"Clary's party, Clary's choice." Riley grinned as Conor tripped and collided into Claron, taking them both down into the tall grass as the cow looked on in unamused disdain.

"This could take hours by the looks of it." Declan leaned his back against the fence and crossed his arms and ankles.

"She won't take feed?"

"Nope." Jaron relaxed next to Declan, none of the brothers even considering helping as Delaney stood watching in awe at what unfolded before them. Murphy just shook his head as he hopped the fence. "And what do you plan to do?"

Murphy turned with a wicked tilt to his lips. "I'm going to get the lass to move." The brothers stood to attention and Riley sat a bit straighter as they watched in refreshed interest as Murphy inched his way towards the cow's behind. Claron and Conor attempted to lure her with feed, with calm tones, with hay, but the cow continued to munch on the grass and stare blankly beyond them, as if she dreamed of the peace she once felt before the crazy men began to bother her. Murphy nodded towards a tired Claron and a panting Conor, both men exhausted from their efforts.

"Don't be stupid, brother," Claron softly warned.

Murphy eased towards the cow and reared back his hand. With a swish, a loud slap sounded on the cow's behind and she burst forth with speed. Claron and Conor dived out of the way as she kicked her back legs into the air. A hoof connected with Murphy's arm and he felt a crunch and a swell of pain as he watched her run towards the opening in the fence she'd escaped through earlier. When she was on the other side, Conor and Claron quickly mended the wires of the fence as Murphy's knees buckled and he landed on the soft grass. He held his right arm and elbow close to his chest as pain blinded him.

Riley and Declan were already running towards him, not able to see where the hoof had landed, they feared he'd been kicked in the chest.

When they reached him and spotted the swelling already increasing the size of his elbow, Declan swatted him on the back of the head. "You're a right, eejit, Murphy, you know that? Bloody Martha. Let's get him up. Aine's going to be steamin' when we bring him in."

Riley helped hoist Murphy to his feet and they escorted him out of the field and loaded him in Riley's truck. Claron followed close behind, both vehicles loaded down with the rest of the crew as they headed towards Shannon hospital.

Delaney, having confiscated one of the bottles of whiskey from the crate, handed it to Murphy. He nodded his thanks as he twisted off the top and took a long swig.

"What were you bloody thinking?" Declan scolded again. "Slappin' a cow from behind, of all things." He ended on a laugh as Murphy began to sing "I'll Tell Me Ma" from the back seat.

"I don't think he's the full shilling right now, brother," Riley chuckled before joining in on the chorus, a pleased Murphy leaning forward and gripping Riley's shoulder in bolstered camaraderie. Murphy looked expectantly at Delaney and the polished Welshman just shook his head in dismay before adding to the melody as well. When Shannon hospital came into view, no one was more grateful than Declan.

When he stepped out of Riley's truck the voices singing inside carried towards the rest of the brothers and Conor as they walked towards them. Claron's face split into an amused smile as Murphy emerged, draping an arm around his shoulders and giving him an affectionate squeeze as he continued the chorus of "The Irish Rover," expecting his brothers and friends to contribute to the accompanying chant.

"I thought the whiskey would help with the pain," Delaney explained. "But it seems it may have turned him into a musical leprechaun."

Conor loudly joined in on the song and Murphy hopped from Claron to his friend as they walked through the doors of the emergency room.

Declan walked to the desk and requested his wife. A few minutes later, a worried Aine hurried into the waiting room. When her eyes fell upon the bulk of the brothers serenading the administrators, she frowned. Hands on hips, she looked to Declan for explanation. Fumbling for what to say or how to explain, he said, "'Twas a cow," and had the rambunctious O'Rifcan clan bursting into laughter.

∞

Piper could hear the laughter pouring out of the salon that held a late-night feast of strawberries, wine, and chocolates as Rhea and the rest of the girls sat in oversized massage chairs and their feet and calves received the royal treatment of scrubs and polish. Chloe had sent her the text of their location, and though she felt like throwing in the towel, it was Rhea's weekend, and Piper did not want to disappoint her friends. She took a deep breath and forced a cheerful smile on her face as she walked inside. "So this is where I find you? Drinking more wine?"

Rhea's face lit up as she waved Piper inside and explained to the manager that she was their last guest. "I'm so glad you could make it. I hope they weren't upset you couldn't stay and work tonight."

Piper gave Chloe a grateful nod for not divulging the reason she was delayed. "He was very understanding, considering the circumstances," Piper reported. "I've a mind to soak my feet though." She pointed to the awaiting chair and accepted the glass of wine on her way to her seat. As she sat, her phone rang. "Ay-yi-yi, sorry Rhea. It seems I can't go anywhere tonight. Oh—"

"What? Who is it?" Heidi asked, noticing the confusion on Piper's face.

"It's Riley."

Heidi's brows rose as she wondered why her boyfriend would be calling Piper.

"Hello there, O'Rifcan," Piper greeted. "And why are you calling me instead of yer— what the devil is that in the background?" She clicked for the call to go to speakerphone and all the women listened.

"That be Murphy," Riley explained. "And Conor, and Clary, and Delaney, and Jaron."

"And they're singing because???" Piper chuckled as a high pitched, off key harmony pierced the air.

"Because Delaney gave Murphy a wee bit too much of the bottle earlier and Murphy demands everyone join in on the chorus." Riley grunted as the phone shuffled from what must have been him almost dropping it. Murphy's cheerful voice filtered through the line. "Piper, me love, I need you now more than ever."

"Dat so?" Amused, Piper listened.

"Aye, lass. Ol' Aine has clipped me wing and I'm a sad sort. I need the help of a master kegsman."

"What do you mean you've clipped your wing?" Rhea called out.

"Oh, Rhea darling," Murphy chimed. "I love you, you know that?"

Rhea just shook her head and rolled her eyes. "Murphy..." she warned. "Tell us what is going on."

"I blame Clary's cow. She bested me. And all I was trying to do was be helpful."

Several voices began clamoring closer and speaking over one another as the brother's tried to report what actually happened. Conor's hearty laugh and ending of "slapped her behind and called it quits," had all the women straightening in their chairs.

"Murphy did what?" Rhea barked, thinking he'd slapped a woman's behind.

A sighing Riley took the phone back. "A cow escaped through the fence earlier and instead of letting Conor and Clary take care of her, Murphy slapped her behind to get her moving. She kicked him. He's a broken elbow and fractured arm. Aine's seen to him. And scolded us all."

"As she should. *Fools.*" Layla looked heavenward as the other women smiled.

"But he is doing alright?" Rhea asked for reassurance.

"Aye. He be grand," Riley assured her. "He won't feel so great in the mornin', but Aine gave him some pain pills should he need them."

"I need to talk to Piper." Murphy's voice flooded over the speaker again.

"You don't have to yell, brother," Riley growled. "I'm right here." He turned his attention back to the women. "He's literally standing right beside me," Riley explained. "What do you need to tell Piper, brother?"

"Tomorrow for the pub. I need her to manage the kegs for me."

"He's actually being serious," Riley reported. "Can you do it, Piper? If not, we can all figure something out, I'm sure. But his first request is you."

"Piper has her own bloody pub to run," Layla yelled from across the room. "And it be girl's weekend. It's Rhea's weekend. Not fair for Piper to be cut short a fun time just because Murphy was acting the fool."

Piper held up her hand for Layla to halt her insults. "I can do it."

The women studied her closely, but none closer than Chloe.

"You sure?" Riley said. "Hate to put this on you last minute."

"It's alright. I don't mind."

"Brilliant. I'll let him know. We'll most likely be wrapping up our shenanigans tonight instead of using the entire weekend. This experience has been more than enough for Clary, I'm afraid. I think he wishes for his peace again." Riley chuckled.

"Then we will wrap up here as well," Rhea told him.

The other women pleaded that it wasn't necessary, but Rhea held up her hand to ward off further comments. "Maybe we can all do a celebratory dinner at Claron's tomorrow evening in place of individual gatherings?"

Layla shrugged. Heidi nodded that it was a passable idea. Chloe smiled in assurance. And Piper felt thankful she had a job, whether it was in Galway or Castlebrook, but no one needed to know of that news yet.

"Sounds like a plan, Rhea darling," Riley finished. "I'll pass the word along to the lads. You lovely lasses have a wonderful rest of your evening. Good bye to me beautiful, Heidi," he called louder before hanging up.

"Well, it looks like this party is going to hit the road tomorrow. I thought you had to work here in Galway tomorrow, Piper?" Heidi asked.

"My boss doesn't need me tomorrow after all," Piper said.

"Fortunate for Murphy. Poor guy." Rhea shook her head but bit back a smile.

"Poor guy?" Layla's eyes widened at the absurdity. "Bloody idiot is more like it. Slapping a cow's behind."

The women laughed.

"I'm sure he had a cheering squad to encourage him," Rhea pointed out.

"Aye, there be some truth to that, I'm sure." Chloe giggled as they all tried to envision the events that must have unfolded. "Are you sure you want to marry into such a brood?" Chloe asked her.

"More than anything," Rhea replied. "More than anything."

«CHAPTER FIVE»

Murphy awoke to a pounding in his head. Rubbing a hand over his face and grimacing at the sliver of light leaking through his curtains, he started to rise from his bed and groaned as pain reminded him of his new annoyance. He tenderly held his arm close to his side as he snatched the sling and wrapped his arm inside and configured it around his back and shoulders. It was but a minute later that he realized it wasn't his head that was pounding, but a fist against his door.

Living on the back side of the pub brought its conveniences, but on mornings when an eager consumer, mainly Seamus, wished to camp out in the pub for most of the day, they knew where to find him. He ran a hand through his blond hair and knew he looked like he'd battled the bottle. Though, when he thought about it, he supposed he had. Unintentionally. He opened the door and Piper stood bright and as fresh as the first ray of the morning sun. She grimaced when she saw him.

"You look a fright." She shouldered past him and into his small efficiency. Her eyes wandered and he hoped he'd not made a mess of things the night before when his brothers brought him home. She turned, hands on hips. "Well, how bad is it?"

He rubbed a hand over his usually trimmed beard and thought it too must have abandoned all hope last night and grown a foot, for he felt ragged.

"And be honest." She held up a finger in warning and he sighed.

"Feels like me bloody arm could be sawed off and I wouldn't have a care if it was. Makes me entire arm, shoulder, neck, and back ache. I feel like I might faint if I accidentally bump it, *and* I'm tired. Is that honest enough for you then?" He sat on the arm of his sofa and Piper's faced turned sympathetic.

"Refreshingly so," she told him. "Have you any pills for the pain?"

"Aye. Somewhere. Not sure where it was placed last night." He went to rise, and she held her hand on his good arm.

"I'll fetch'em. Have a seat on the sofa there."

He heard her rummaging in his kitchen and the sound of the tap. She brought him two pills and a glass of water. "Says to take every four hours or when needed."

"So the whole bottle now then?"

She chuckled as she sat next to him, studying the side of his face as he leaned his head back and closed his eyes.

"You can say it," he told her, and his lips slightly tilted, though he didn't look at her.

"Say what?"

"What I know you're thinking."

"And what might that be? Are you a mind reader now then? A new talent?"

He grunted. "You think me a fool."

"Oh, aye, all the time," she agreed and he turned his bright blue eyes on her. She smirked. "But did the cow go back through the fence?"

"She did."

"Then I'd say you were a helpful fool."

He chuckled. "I like your spin on things, Piper O'Beirne. Now cheer me up with tales of the women's wild night? Was it full of shenanigans and malarkey?"

Piper snorted. "Not quite. Though I had to miss a portion of it."

"Why's that?" His brow rose in curiosity and at her bitter tone.

Not wanting to reveal more than necessary, Piper shrugged. "Work."

"I thought you took the night off?"

"I did, but something came up. It wasn't for long though."

"That why yer boss be giving you today off then?"

"Not quite." Not elaborating and staring into his blank television, she knew he looked at her expectantly.

"I thank you for coming to my aid today. I know it's not what you planned."

She turned and faced him, resting her face in her hand and elbow on the back of the sofa. "I enjoy working here in Castlebrook."

"But not enough to work here full time," he pointed out.

"I've been thinking on that too."

"Have you now?" He angled his face towards hers and waited for her to explain.

"I just received a raise in Galway, it's why I've been hesitant."

"Whatever it is, I'll match it," Murphy challenged. "And then some, if necessary."

She heaved an exasperated sigh and just shook her head. "Why me, Murphy?"

"What do you mean, why you? You're bloody brilliant. You've experience. A good head on yer shoulders. You're trustworthy. Not to mention you work hard. How am I doing?" he asked.

She grinned. "You could keep going, but that would just be me being selfish."

He laughed and then groaned as the movement had his arm aching.

"Easy now." She leaned towards him and he smelled her sweet perfume. Her hands delicately lifted his arm and she slid a pillow under his elbow. His free hand reached up and tucked silky strands of her hair behind her ear. The action taking her off guard, she pulled back quickly from his touch. "You should ice it."

"Aye. I plan to eventually. Seeing as to how you woke me up this mornin', I have yet to make it very far in my duties for the day."

"I could make you a pack," she offered.

"That's okay. I've stolen more of your time today than is necessary. I do want you to know I did talk to me Mam, and you've your usual room at the B&B when you work me pub. No charge."

"I can't keep taking up space and not pay."

"Don't argue." Murphy, tired, laid his head back again. "I've got Riley lined up to cover the pub Sunday evening. I've still to figure out the rest after that but hoping Tommy can fill in a few days."

"I can do it. I can work all weekend and next week."

He eyed her again, his brow wrinkling. "What are you not telling me?"

She fidgeted and he immediately knew she was holding back something. "Nothing."

"Liar."

Her hackles rose and her cheeks colored. "Don't call me a liar. You know nothing of me life or schedule."

He held up his free hand in surrender. "Something be wrong and you're withholding from me. I get it, but if you are in some sort of trouble, I need to know."

"Trouble? And what trouble would I be in?" Piper countered, offended he might think less of her character.

"I don't know. That's why I'm asking." Murphy sat up and faced her. "Tell me, because you look guiltier than a nun who's just betrayed her vows."

"Gee. Thanks."

"Piper—" he prodded.

"Alright... I left the pub in Galway."

His eyes widened in surprise. "But you said you just got a raise."

"I did."

"Then why leave?"

"There were other factors."

"What sort of other factors?"

"Just... other factors, Murphy. Why do you have to be the nosiest man I've ever bloody met?" She stormed to his kitchen and he heard cabinets banging closed as she searched for something. He prayed it was more water.

She walked back into the room carrying an ice pack made of a storage bag and cubes from his ice trays. She wrapped it in a dish towel and laid it over his elbow.

"Well thanks for that." He saw the remorse in her eyes at losing her temper. "Talk to me, love. Tell me your woes." He patted the cushion next to him.

"I can't." Piper inched closer to the door.

"Don't be runnin' out on me just yet, Piper darling. I've just spent the majority of my time with all me brothers, Conor, and Delaney. I need some female attention for a wee bit. Besides, I'm pitiful. And wouldn't that just be rude to leave me in such a state?"

She rolled her eyes as he grinned.

"Fine. A few minutes more." She sat beside him on the couch once again.

"Now, talk."

"I can't."

"Really? Again? You're going to have to give me more than that. And yes, I'm nosy. But I'm also yer friend, and I'd like to help, if I can."

"No one can help. It's been like this for years."

"What's been like this?"

Their eyes held for a long silent minute and Murphy hoped she'd trust him with whatever secret or burden she carried. When her shoulders relaxed, he knew she finally did.

"My father."

He raised a brow for her to continue.

"He's a bit of a— How do I put this nicely? Scoundrel."

"He be troubling you?"

"Always," she scoffed. "He doesn't know any better it seems."

"We always know better," Murphy told her. "What's he doing?"

"He has a problem with the bottle and with bets. Every now and then when he's up to his neck in debts he can't pay, he comes to me work and causes a scene until I escort him home, pay his debts, and leave him be. Only this time my boss had had enough. Can't blame him really, my boss.

Me Nan will be beside herself over the notion of me losing my work, but I'll assure her I will be fine. I *will* be fine. I always am."

Murphy reached for her hand and was pleased to see she didn't withdraw from his touch. He laced his fingers with hers. "Your Nan, she sounds like a nice lass."

"Oh, aye. She is. She pretty much raised me since me Da was such a vagrant."

"Sounds like a tough woman herself. No wonder you're a strong one."

She smiled appreciatively at him. "She is. I hate that she feels obligated to take care of him. I don't understand her commitment, but then again, what am I doing but the very same thing? At the end of the day, whether I like it or not, he's family. And I wouldn't be able to live with myself if something happened to him because I didn't do what I could to help him."

"A tough situation to be sure." Murphy pondered it a moment. "Your Nan be in Galway, I assume."

"Aye. Another reason I haven't moved to Castlebrook. I hate not being close enough to help her out."

"'Tis not too far a drive, really," Murphy continued, his mind spinning thinking of ways to work out the situation for Piper's benefit and his own. "Has your Da tried a treatment center?"

"Several times. But it's never lasted."

"Arrested?"

"Several times."

He squeezed her hand and he saw the moment their connection registered on her face. She unwound her fingers from his and stood.

"I can work for your pub, Murphy, but we may need to negotiate scheduling so I can see to Nan when need be."

"That be an easy enough request, but are you sure you want to do this? Move to Castlebrook?"

"I won't be moving just yet. I will just commute."

"That's absurd, Piper. It's too far a drive to do every day. Especially at the wee hours of the mornin'. All I'd do is fret."

"Right." She rolled her eyes and then grew serious when she saw he wasn't kidding. "Well, I'll ease your worries today and stay at your mam's. But if I'm to be here often I wish to pay her for my room."

"That can be arranged." He shifted the ice pack off his arm and grunted as he attempted to stand.

"Don't get up," she told him. "I know my way."

"'Tis not unlocked yet."

"Where's your key?"

He pointed to a hook by the entry. No keys rested there. "Blast!" he growled. "Maybe Declan has them." He surveyed his living room for his phone and saw it resting on the bar of the kitchen next to his ring of keys. "Ah, there." He pointed.

She fetched them. "Got them. Now prop yer arm, ice it, and rest. I've got the pub covered." She walked towards the door and Murphy followed. When she stepped out and turned back to face him for a final farewell, she smiled. "Thanks for listening and understanding, Murphy. I'm not proud of what me Da does or how he lives, and I'm fairly ashamed of it, to be honest. But I appreciate you understanding my need to see to Nan."

"Family is important. No matter how grand or how non grand they may be. I'm glad you told me." He brushed his finger over her smooth cheek, the action causing her to take a cautious step back.

"I think your pain pills are kicking in, Romeo," she chuckled as she raised his keys. "See you later. Rest."

He watched her round the corner and already missed her company. Piper's news of her father and nan surprised him, but he couldn't be anything but proud of the woman she was despite her family situation. She was strong, kind, and beautiful. He rubbed a hand over his scruffy face and groaned as he shut his door. The last thing he needed to do was think she was beautiful. Not Piper. Not anyone. But most definitely not Piper. When he sat on his couch and pulled the ice back onto his arm, he sighed as he closed his eyes, and much to his pretended disappointment, all he pictured was Piper.

∞

She had an hour before the door was to open and Piper prepped the bar and did last minute checks of the keg connections. *Poor Murphy*, she thought with a smile. The man was a fool for thinking he could slap a cow, but the fact he was brave enough to try it increased her opinion of him. He was a helpful lad. And she could just picture him wanting to be of help to Clary and Conor, while also wishing to make the others laugh. She shook her head as she straightened a toppling glass before it fell to the ground. Her cell phone ring twittered through the air and she looked down to see her nan calling.

"Mornin', Nan."

"Piper, dear." The warmth of Nan's voice always calmed Piper. A haven of comfort on days she needed it most. "Yer father had a go at a Garda this mornin'. He's being detained."

Piper pinched the bridge of her nose. "This mornin'?"

"Aye. He was in a major tizzy last night when the cabbie dropped him off. Said you all but tossed him out of the pub."

"I escorted him out," Piper corrected. "And he was drunk and disrupting the peace."

"Oh, I believe it," Nan assured her. "What do we do?"

Sighing, Piper sat on a stool. "I don't know, Nan. I just don't know anymore. Perhaps it will be good for 'im to stew a bit."

"I've wondered the same. Though I hate to do it."

"I know what you mean. I can't pick him up right now any way. I'm in Castlebrook running the pub for Murphy today and this evening."

"Seems you're in Castlebrook most of the time these days. Anything I should know? Are you staying with the lad?"

"Oh heavens no." Piper laughed at the idea of her and Murphy, though inwardly the idea didn't seem as preposterous as before. "He's hurt himself, broken elbow. Just needs an extra hand for a bit."

"And what of your job here?"

Piper quieted and her Nan continued. "Ah, I see. Last night was the end of that, wasn't it? I'm so sorry, dearie. I know how much you loved yer work."

"It isn't the first job I've lost because of Da. I'm sure it won't be the last."

"Don't say that," Nan scolded. "A person can always change."

Feeling guilty, Piper exhaled on a shaky breath. "So, should I fetch him from the cell?"

"No. Just because I don't want you giving up hope on yer Da doesn't mean I want you to cater to him. We'll let him sit and think of his wrongdoings for however long they'll hold him. 'Tis time for him to see he can't be bullying us around with his habits."

"Aye, I know you're right, Nan, but 'tis always hard."

"I know, love. I know. 'Tis a burden neither of us should have ever had to bear, especially you. I think it grand you have a job at this Murphy's pub to see you through until you decide your next step. Who knows? Perhaps it will be a good fit."

"But it's in Castlebrook," Piper reminded her. "Not Galway."

"And what be wrong with that?" Murphy's voice carried from the doorway and he grinned. "Not earwigging, just heard your last comment. Deeply offended, I am, by the way." He held his free hand to his chest. "As if Castlebrook isn't as lovely as Galway." He tsked his tongue.

"What are you doing here? I left you resting." Piper eyed him curiously.

"I'm lonely all by myself." Murphy motioned towards her phone and she blanched realizing Nan was still on the line.

"So sorry, Nan. Murphy just walked into the pub. He's supposed to be resting."

"Ah, the lovely Nan, is it?" Murphy asked. "Give her my best."

Piper looked heavenward as she turned back to her conversation with her grandmother.

"He sounds lovely," Nan commented.

"He has his moments," Piper replied, and had Murphy raising a curious brow. "Listen, I need to get to work, especially if my new boss insists on hovering."

"Oh, be fair now, Piper." Murphy spoke loudly so Nan could hear as well. "I'm not hoverin'. Just in need of some lovely company while I'm injured."

"Keep the boy company, Piper," Nan ordered on a laugh. "Sounds like he's a happy sort that needs a bit of social interaction."

"Aye. That be the truth of it. I love you. I will talk with you later. Have a care." She hung up and swiveled to face Murphy. "Why are you here, really?"

Murphy shrugged, the action causing a brief expression of discomfort to wash over his face. "I can't sit around my house and do nothing, Piper. I need to feel useful. I know I can't do much, but I can entertain my guests."

"That's true enough. Perhaps seeing you relaxed while I'm overseeing the bar will show them I'm capable and that you trust me to run things."

"I do trust you."

"Aye, but your customers don't fully respect me, as was evident the other day. Perhaps they will now."

"Good point. Well, there's not much I can do until the gang arrives. I think I'm going to venture to Clary's and continue hanging with the boys for a bit."

"No slapping cows' behinds," she warned.

He laughed. "I've learned me lesson on that one."

"That's good to hear." Piper stood and walked him to the door of the pub.

"Can I bring you anything back?"

Her brows rose. "What could I need?"

"Food," he said. "From me mam's or McCarthy's."

"Ah. I could go for whatever your mam has whipped up for the day. But no rush. Enjoy your day."

He playfully tugged a strand of her short hair, his knuckles brushing against her jawline. "Done. See you in a bit."

She watched as he began whistling and meandering his way up the sidewalk. She saw him pause and knock on the window of his sisters' shop and wave before continuing on. She wasn't sure which sister was working, probably Chloe. Though everyone agreed to meet at the pub for the evening to finish off the celebratory weekend, wedding plans were still on the to-do list. Chloe had her hands full receiving flowers and making the arrangements. They had two weeks until the big day, and she knew Chloe had received the vases for the centerpieces. Conor had built the infamous arch that Chloe was somehow planning to decorate on one leg. Layla had designed the programs and organized the flow of events. And Sidna and Mrs. McCarthy had partnered on the reception menu. Murphy had agreed to supply the drinks. An order, she realized, she hadn't seen the ticket for. She wondered if he'd placed a supply order yet and made a mental note to ask him. All that was needed now was for the day to arrive. A tap sounded on the door and a couple of faces peered through their hands to see if anyone stood at the bar. They waved when they spotted Piper. She glanced at the clock, *half an hour until opening time.* Shrugging, she walked to the door and opened it in welcome. "Come on in, lads. Let me fetch ye a pint."

«CHAPTER SIX»

Murphy traded his legs for his truck when he decided to ride out to Claron's and see what his brothers and friends had been up to since the night before, but when he arrived it was only Claron, Roland, Paul, and his da sitting on Clary's back porch.

He paused under the awning. "Did you run them all off, brother?"

Clary turned and held up an iced glass of lemonade in salute before motioning to a chair next to him. "All are resting for now. In their own beds, minus Riley, who is currently in my guest room."

"I see you've rounded up the second posse." Murphy slapped a friendly hello on his father's shoulder as he eased into the chair.

"Celebrating isn't only for the young," Claron Senior jested. "Me boyo is getting married. I like soaking up the moments just like the lot of ye. How's the arm, lad?"

"A total buggar," Murphy admitted. "Been giving me fits all mornin'. But darling Piper fed me my pills and ordered me to rest, so it's only a matter of time until I'm back to full swing."

"A good lass, that Piper," Senior added.

"Aye. Handy in a tight spot," Murphy agreed.

"A pretty little fairy, is she not?" Senior continued and had Claron biting back a smile as he sipped his lemonade. The matchmaking wheels did not reside only in their mother's brain, but also their father's.

"Aye, and a wee bit of sass and stubbornness to pack a punch."

"Those are the best kind," Roland interrupted.

Murphy looked to Claron. "Any more of that?" He motioned towards Claron's glass.

"Aye. I'll fetch you one, brother." Claron stood and headed into the cottage.

"And Paul, how is our darling Jeanie on this fine mornin'?" Murphy looked to Rhea's father and he sighed, comfortably resting against the back of his own seat.

"Helping your mother. Apparently all the ladies are taste-testing cake flavors this morning."

"All except Chloe," Murphy pointed out. "Saw her with her flowers on my way."

"Where she is happiest." Roland smiled lovingly.

"Aye," Murphy agreed. "Though I'm surprised Conor wasn't lurking in her shadow."

His father grinned. "The boyo loves her so. How we never thought of that match is beyond me. Sidna must be getting rusty."

"Don't tell her that," Roland chuckled and had all the men smiling.

"With Piper under her roof, it won't be long before she's intentions for the lass to marry one of you," Senior warned. "Best be prepared."

"Jaron is apparently seeing a lass. Jace as well. Tommy is free as of late, a wee bit depressed, but perhaps a potential for Mam to hover over." Murphy looked up as Claron walked out carrying a lemonade for him and handed it to him.

"Riley's awake. He'll be out in a few," Claron reported.

"I'm surprised he and Heidi are separated at the moment." Murphy took a sip of his drink and swished the soothing sweet and tart mixture around in his mouth before swallowing. Clary had an impeccable skill when it came to lemonade.

"Jealous, brother?" Claron asked with a smirk.

"Not a'tall."

"Liar." All the other men said in unison and then laughed.

Murphy gawked at them. "You think I'm jealous of all you lovesick puppies runnin' about? Having to prep the cottage for a ceremony? Having to taste a thousand cakes? Or worry about suits and dresses? I think not."

"Do you see me running?" Claron asked him. "I'm sitting right here, enjoying the day with some of me favorite lads, relaxed, happy, and in love with the most beautiful woman in the world. Who, by the way, I get the honor of marrying soon. And who I will come home to every day and wake up to every mornin'. I could think of nothing better than that."

Paul lightly dabbed his eyes at hearing Claron speak of Rhea. The father of the bride turned his head so as not to draw attention to himself, but Murphy caught the pleased and proud expression on the man's face before he attempted to fade into the background. And blast, that he didn't wish to have the same feelings Clary did for someone. But he wasn't in a hurry. Just because he wanted it all someday didn't mean he had to have feelings for someone right at that very moment.

"Food for thought," Roland stated, tapping Murphy's knee as the back door opened and a disheveled Riley shuffled out.

"Ah, sleeping beauty has awakened." Murphy looked up at his brother and smiled.

"I see you're managing." Riley nodded towards Murphy's sling.

"Aye. Painful as the day is long, but I'll survive."

"Good to hear. Heidi reamed me for not intervening on behalf of your stupidity."

"Oh, Heidi my love. Worried about me, is she?"

"Don't get cocky," Riley smirked. "I believe her exact words were that it served you right, but that we all should have received kicks in the head for not behaving like grown men."

"Always the subtle one, your lass." Murphy grinned as Riley planted himself on a stool near the door.

"Piper managing the kegs?" Riley asked.

"Aye. Which reminds me. You're off the hook, brother. I've won Piper over to Castlebrook. She is now employed full time and can manage the pub all week."

Riley and Claron's brows rose in surprise.

"What made her decide to make the move?" Claron asked.

Knowing, but also understanding Piper would not want anyone to know of her father and the loss of her last job, he just shrugged. "It was all my charmin' her, I'm sure."

Senior scoffed. "You, boyo, best treat the lass with respect."

"I do. I am. And I will. I'm thankful for her. No better person for the job."

"And where she be living?" Riley asked.

"She'll be staying at the B&B with Mam and Da." Murphy nodded towards his father. "I've already sorted it with Mam and covered the costs for the meantime."

"Does Piper know that?" Riley asked.

"She knows she is staying there, yes."

"But not about you footing the bill?"

"That would be a no. And she won't." He narrowed his gaze at his brothers. "She already feels she's taking advantage of Mam's kindness for letting her stay there. I do not wish for her to learn I've been paying her fees since she's been helping me."

"She's helped you for over six months." Claron's eyes widened. "You've paid her fees to Mam all this time?"

"Aye. Why shouldn't I?" Murphy asked.

"Well, most employees just work and go home to a place they pay for themselves, whether a home or a hotel," Riley pointed out.

"It's my arrangement." Murphy stated with an edge to his voice. "And it suits Mam and gives her compensation for a room. I do not wish for her to miss out on extra wages because I have a friend needing a place to stay. Roland paid Rhea's fees, I'll pay Piper's."

"A friend, is she?" Riley prodded.

"Aye. And one to you as well," Murphy countered.

"And two seconds ago she was just an employee."

"She can be both, Riley, now stop being a nuisance." Murphy set his glass down on the ground and stood. "I think I'm having a hankering for some cake or more pills. Me arm is starting to hate me. So I think I will head to the B&B and let all your women fret over me a bit and then head home for some rest before tonight."

"Could have your own woman to fret over ye," Senior presented.

"But why, when all of yours' do it so well?" Murphy winked. "I'll give Rhea and Heidi your best." He tossed a wave at his annoyed brothers and headed towards his truck with a satisfied smirk. When he eased behind the wheel, he allowed himself a brief moment to absorb the pain he felt throbbing in his elbow. Gasping for a quick breath, he gripped the steering wheel until it passed. Cake may have to wait. Suddenly the only appetite he had was for more pain medication and a long rest.

∞

Piper looked up at the sound of womanly chatter and the friendly faces of Rhea and the remaining O'Rifcan women. Heidi brought up the rear carrying three large bakery boxes while Layla carried two smaller ones. Rhea set her purse on the bar and grinned. "Since you are working, we brought the party to you."

Grateful, Piper smiled. "Did you now? No party without me, is it?"

Rhea chuckled. "Well, we are tasting cake samples. Thought it might be fun to get everyone's opinion. It's a pretty slow day, isn't it?" Rhea looked around the pub.

"Yes, thankfully. Just have the two playing checkers and one in the corner mindin' his own."

"Good. We passed Murphy. He said he was going to follow the scent and join us."

"Of course he did."

Rhea grinned. "O'Rifcans can't sit still, Piper. Prime example." She pointed to Chloe who hobbled her way to a table and eased into a chair, adjusting her leg brace and leaning her crutches against the wall.

"Murphy said she was in her shop earlier."

"Yep. We kidnapped her." Rhea beamed proudly.

Heidi walked the boxes over to the table and set them down before coming back to the bar. "Does Murphy keep any champagne back there?" The voluptuous brunette leaned atop the bar as she waited for Piper to fetch them some.

"Indeed, he does." Murphy's voice carried to them as he walked forward and planted a kiss on Rhea's cheek and then slid his arm around Heidi's waist. "But only for a kiss."

She pinched his cheek and lightly slapped it.

"That will work too." He grinned and she laughed. "I'll fetch you ladies a couple of bottles."

"No. You won't," Piper scolded. "I will. You need to sit." She pointed to the table with the boxes as Layla began cutting into the first mini cake for them to all sample.

"As you command." Murphy winked at Rhea and Heidi as he meandered towards his sisters.

"Is he being a handful?" Rhea asked.

"Not really," Piper answered. "He just won't sit still. I don't think he realizes rest is just as important as that sling on his arm. But I have a feeling I will be blue in the face before that point is driven home."

Rhea reached across the bar and squeezed her hand, her brown eyes dancing. "Hang in there. He's grateful you're here, and he is listening to you. He's just pretending he isn't."

Piper rolled her eyes. "Eejit."

"Always," Heidi added with a smirk. "But ya gotta love him."

The women chuckled as Murphy held up a plate with a slice of cake on it. "This be the one, Rhea. I'm certain of it."

"Is that the first one you've tried?" Rhea asked.

"Aye."

"Then it's not the one yet, Murphy." She laughed as she headed towards the table and sat. Murphy forked off a piece of the cake and fed it to her.

Her brows rose. "Oh, that is lovely."

"It has me vote as of right now," Murphy told her.

"Let's try another one." Rhea's eyes greedily took in the remaining miniature cakes and Chloe laughed.

"Pace yourself, Rhea, or you'll be having a sore stomach."

"I can't help it. They all look so delicious."

Piper walked towards the table with champagne and glasses. Murphy accepted the bottle from her and began working on the cork. As he twisted the wires, the cork didn't release. With his one hand, he aimed the bottle away from everyone and nudged the cork with his thumb. A loud pop sounded, and Piper held the first glass for him to pour. He handed it to Rhea. "For the bride."

She accepted the glass and did a small dance in her chair in excitement. He smiled as he passed the remaining glasses around. He handed one to Piper. "I can't drink, I'm working," she told him.

"And I'm your boss. Just keep your head about you and you'll be fine. If anything, just join in on the toast."

Sighing, but acquiescing, Piper held her glass as Murphy began a speech.

"To our darling, lovely Rhea. For the life of all of us O'Rifcans, we cannot figure out what she sees in our brother, Clary, but are supremely grateful she chose him. You're a light for him and for us. And the love you two share is beautiful to behold. May you grow old and gray and forever be cherished." He raised his glass. "To Rhea."

"To Rhea," they all replied, raising their glasses in toast.

Rhea patted Murphy's knee as she swiped away a tear. "You always know exactly what to say, Murphy."

He leaned towards her. "Then let me add this. 'Tis not too late, Rhea. Just say the word and I shall sweep you off your feet." His wicked little grin had her laughing and had Layla reaching over and slapping him upside the head. He grunted. "Layla, can't you see I'm bloody injured?"

"Yer arm, yes. Your confidence on the other hand..."

The women laughed. Piper took a quick sip of her drink and walked back to the bar. She could feel Murphy watching her. When she caught his gaze, he raised his glass to her and winked before turning his attention to the next slice of cake.

Rhea was a lucky woman to be marrying into such a loving family. To be a part of a family that had fun together, teased one another, and respected one another. The O'Rifcans were just as rare a find as sweet Rhea. Not all families operated like they did. Though they had their squabbles, in the short time Piper had known them, she'd never seen them argue for long. Instead, they seemed to genuinely enjoy each other's company while still treating one another as siblings. Annoying one another. Being a bit too nosy for their own good at times. She couldn't fathom ever having such a family dynamic. And she doubted whether, if she did, she'd know how to maintain such. Her experience was rougher, less rosy. Grayer. And not that she felt sorry for herself— because she didn't thanks to Nan— but she wasn't quite sure if she'd ever belong to a family like the O'Rifcans. She'd never fit in because of the baggage she carried. Her father would always be a burden with extra costs, and no man, no matter how wonderful, would ever want to take that on.

So, she'd watch from afar. Observe and celebrate the merging of two wonderful people. Two wonderful families. And she'd be happy for them. Simple enough. But Murphy glanced her way again and held up his plate, his eyes light with pleasure as he beckoned her forward. "You have to sample this one, Piper. It's me favorite."

"I thought the last one was your favorite?" Chloe asked him.

""Tis a grand tie. I'll just have to sample them each again."

Piper walked forward and he held up his fork. She hesitated a moment, his brow rising in curiosity as he wondered whether she'd accept his offering. When the fork slipped in her mouth and the sweet flavors of vanilla, amaretto, and cream exploded on her tongue, her eyes sparked. An answering grin spread over Murphy's face as he watched her. Their faces were close as she sampled, and the sisters and Rhea not only watched for her reaction to the cake but the interaction between she and Murphy.

"Wow." Piper leaned back and dabbed her lips with a napkin, Murphy watching her every move. "That is delicious. It has my vote."

Rhea looked happily at Murphy, but she paused a moment when she saw the brother still staring at Piper as if seeing her in a new light. Rhea's lips twitched as she nudged Heidi beside her and nodded towards his direction. The sisters, aware of the women staring at their brother, caught his trance as well.

"Earth to cowboy." Heidi tossed her balled up napkin hitting Murphy in the chest. He flinched and focused on the rest of the table.

"Aye. Bring on the next one."

"You sure?" Heidi tilted her head and lightly bit her bottom lip to cover her smile. "You sure seemed to like that last... taste."

Clearing his throat and avoiding Heidi, he leaned forward and peered into the box. "Which one is next?"

Rhea, sensing his discomfort, thanked Piper for helping them out and then fished the next flavor from the box.

∞

Her feet were on fire as she slipped her shoes off and tucked them away under the desk nearest the door and made her way towards the bath. Her room at Sidna's B&B was comfort at its finest. Homey touches of potpourri spread about, Chloe's flower bouquets resting on the mantle of the small fireplace and on several tabletops. Piper had a glad eye for the full bed with handmade quilt that awaited her, but she knew a hot bath would do her feet and lower back wonders. Sidna knew how to make her guests feel comfortable. The rooms. The food. The *glorious* food. The mother hen had come to leaving Piper a plate warming in the oven for when she came in at night. And though it was always the wee hours of the morning, Piper indulged and ate every bite and crumb. Again, the O'Rifcan warmth and welcome seeped into her as she slipped into the steamy bath.

She'd consumed her fair share of cake as well. Having to sample each slice, Heidi had occupied one of the chalkboards by the dartboards, keeping a tally on which flavor received the most votes. Various patrons helped in the sampling as well, all of which Rhea found amusing and exciting. Murphy provided his banter and charm to all who entered, and what had started as a slow evening, had picked up pace and kept Piper moving most of the night. Not that she was complaining. She loved the activity of the pub. The chatter, the music, the laughter. It was her happy place to be around joy. She often wondered why a pub of all places was her choice for a safe place considering her father's terrible habits, but perhaps it was so she could exercise some control over it all. She could not control her father's consumption, but she could manage others'. She could modify, encourage, and even help those who might need it. After the Seamus situation, the man had returned and apologized for his behavior. And since that evening, he'd been acting like the model patron. Whatever Murphy or Declan or a cell had done, the man was reevaluating his lifestyle. He'd even showered and shaved, sported a new shirt, *or perhaps it was just clean*, each time he came into the pub. That's the turnaround that made Piper proud. It also made her angry, though she didn't like to admit it. If she, in some small way, can help a stranger, why could she not help her own father? She reached for her phone and dialed Nan.

Despite the ungodly hour, Nan always answered. She was used to Piper's schedule and no matter the time, her grandmother took her call.

"Piper, everything alright, love?"

Just the sound of her voice brought a smile to her face. "Aye. Just wanted to hear your voice, Nan."

"You sound tired. Long day?"

"You could say that, but it was fun. Any word on Da?"

A heavy sigh flooded the line. "Don't be angry with me, Piper," Nan began. "But I failed. I fetched him from the Garda."

Disappointed, but also understanding, Piper sighed. "I understand, Nan. I've been plagued by thought on it all day as well. Did he have any words of regret?"

"No. He's rather upset with us actually. He was even more upset to find you weren't in Galway."

"Thanks to him," Piper pointed out.

"That's exactly what I told him. That you were working at a new pub since he aided in your dismissal from the last one."

"I'm sure he did not take that well."

"No, I'm afraid he didn't. He stormed away and I haven't seen him the rest of the day or night. I haven't heard him come home either."

"So, he is more than likely sitting in a pub drowning his woes."

"Unfortunately."

"I don't know what to do anymore, Nan."

"Don't you worry on it. I can handle him."

"You shouldn't have to, especially not alone."

"Piper lass, listen to me. Don't you go feelin' sorry for me or feeling guilty. You take care of you. Enjoy your new job. If I need you, I will tell you. Is that a fair deal?"

Hesitant, Piper agreed. "'Tis fair. I'd rather you come stay with me here for a bit."

"Oh, now dearie, I'd only be in the way."

"Actually, I think you would love it here. Sidna is absolutely wonderful and I know she'd appreciate the company."

"I can't intrude," Nan continued.

"You can share a room with me. Wouldn't be the first time." Piper's voice warmed at the memory of snuggling next to Nan when she was a wee lass. Nan was who she ran to when she was frightened or needed loving.

"I'll think on it."

"I can have you here later today, if you wish to come. You can go back at any time."

"Desperate, are we?" Nan chuckled.

"You said yourself you've no idea where Da's wandered off to. Why must you wait for him? Come, Nan. Just for a bit. For me."

A long pause silenced the line. "Alright, I'll come for a visit. But how am I to reach you? I've no car. I borrowed the lad's next door to fetch your Da."

"I'll arrange a man named Riley to fetch you. He's Murphy's brother. He's in Galway for work most days. I'll have him swing by after work and pick you up."

"Oh, I hate to put the lad out of his way."

"You aren't. He'll gladly do it. And he'll enjoy every second of your company. Have a bag ready, Nan."

"I will, dearie. I will. Can't wait to see you in your new spot."

"Aye. I'm ready to see you. Have a care, Nan."

"Night, love."

Piper stared at the phone a moment before tears began rolling down her cheeks. Angry that she let her father upset her, she swiped them away and then splashed her face with water. She made a mental note to ask Riley to pick up her grandmother. She hoped he had a reason to be in Galway. If not, she'd simply ask Murphy for a couple of hours to go and fetch her. Pleased that Nan would have the opportunity to live in such comfort as Sidna's B&B and see the beauty of Castlebrook, Piper hoped she might convince her Nan to join her permanently. They could find a house or a flat, she was sure of it. Her heart slowly mending from the day's disappointments of her father's behavior, she slipped out of the tub and hurried into her night clothes to enjoy a long-awaited sleep.

«CHAPTER SEVEN»

Murphy leaned back in his chair and listened to the hustle and bustle of his mam's café at the peek hour of lunch time. Roland sat across from him and Chloe to his right. They'd just finished their meals when Murphy's phone buzzed. He fished in his pant pocket and swiped his thumb over the screen.

"Hello there, brother. What's the story?"

Riley's voice carried over the line. "I'm just reaching Castlebrook. Where are you?"

"Mam's. Just wrapped up a nice bite with Roland and our little coppertop. Why?"

"Be there in a few." Riley hung up and Murphy stared at his phone.

"Something the matter?" Chloe asked, taking a sip of her glass of water.

"Not sure. That was an odd conversation. Riley's coming in from Galway, should be here in a minute or so... looking for me."

"Perhaps he missed you." Chloe giggled at the absurdity and Murphy tugged one of her curls.

"The only person who be missing me is probably Piper, and only because I am of no help to her and she's having to carry the pub on her own."

"Piper can carry herself," Roland stated.

Murphy nodded in agreement. "'Tis true enough." He watched as Roland's face lifted into a warm smile and the older man slowly rose to his feet. Murphy looked over his shoulder to see Riley escorting an older woman dressed in pale pink capris and a whimsical white blouse. Her hair was short, faint white streaks shimmered throughout the blonde that must have once been radiant. Murphy stood as well.

"This be him?" The woman looked up at Riley for confirmation, her eyes showing everyone the brother had been his usual charming self and had another woman wrapped around his finger.

"Aye. He's not much to look at, but he's somewhat of a mind in there," Riley teased, and had her laughing. She removed her arm from his and walked towards Murphy, her hands outstretched as she cupped his face and kissed his cheek.

"Bless you, lad, for giving my Piper a place to work."

"Nan?" Murphy asked.

She chuckled. "Aye, that's me. And though I don't mind you calling me Nan, my name is Evelyn."

"Evelyn." Murphy's usual charming self vanished as he fidgeted on his feet. This was Piper's grandmother and here he sat on his laurels while her granddaughter worked his pub.

"Nice to meet you, boyo." Her eyes fluttered to Chloe. "You must be Chloe." She walked forward and hugged Chloe tightly. "I only know because Piper mentioned your beautiful hair."

Chloe smiled. "That be nice of her." Beaming, Chloe motioned towards Roland. "This be Roland Conners. He is Rhea's grandfather and has been an O'Rifcan for more than me entire life."

Roland patted Chloe's arm appreciatively as he extended his hand towards Evelyn. Evelyn patted her hair before stepping forward and accepting his handshake. Riley's brow rose in amusement as they watched the old man flush at the woman's attention.

He nudged Murphy's arm and pointed to the flustered older couple. Chloe stood between them and engaged them in conversation. "It would seem our Roland still has his charms," Riley whispered.

Murphy looked to Riley. "So why did you bring Nan to me? What is she even doing here?"

"I was asked. Evelyn wished to meet you first before seeing Piper."

"Why?"

"I don't know, brother. I just agreed." Riley looked baffled as to why he should know all the answers. At his answer, Evelyn stepped towards Murphy.

"I wished to know the young man who's been so good to her," Evelyn explained.

Murphy's cheeks reddened as he shook his head. "Piper be the lifesaver." He pointed at his elbow.

"I heard about that too." Nan winked at him. "Slapping a cow?"

Chloe snickered as Murphy had the decency to look embarrassed.

"There's a story in there," Murphy clarified. "More than the fact that I'm a fool."

"I look forward to hearing it." Evelyn looked to Chloe. "I was hoping for a few flowers to take to Piper. I hear you have a charming shop?"

Chloe straightened as Roland handed her crutches over. "Aye. I was just headed back to it if you want to follow along."

"Yes, please." Evelyn looked to Riley. "Thank you for the ride, dearie. You were most delightful." She kissed his cheek. "Now, one more favor."

"At your service, lovely."

"Take your sister to her shop." She pointed at Chloe's leg. "She does not need to trudge her way through the village."

Riley chuckled as he nodded to Chloe. "Aye. You're right about that. She'd do it, too."

Evelyn linked her arm with Murphy's. "I'll have your brother escort me. We'll be along shortly." She turned towards Roland. "It was a pleasure meeting you, Roland. I look forward to seeing you again."

Speechless and not his usual chatty self, Roland nodded sheepishly.

Tugging Murphy onward, they fell into step and began walking up the footpath.

"I don't know where to walk, so you'll have to lead me to our destination."

Murphy smiled. "You seem to be doing well enough. Though it's not far. Just up here a-ways, and the pub is just on the corner there." He pointed. "Will be a nice surprise for Piper, having you here."

"Oh, it's not a surprise. She arranged it all."

"She did?" He looked at her in surprise, his gaze narrowing as he surveyed the side of her face. "Everything alright in Galway?"

She glanced his way a moment before facing forward once again. "Piper told me she shared a bit about our situation with you."

Murphy gave a small nod.

"I will admit I was a bit surprised. She's never shared that with anyone that I know of... not really any way. Her former boss only knew because her father stopped by several times to create a ruckus."

"Aye, she told me that as well."

Evelyn took her turn and studied the side of his face as they walked. He was a handsome lad, but Piper had informed her all the O'Rifcans were stunners. Though she'd only met three of them so far, Evelyn had to agree. "She's nervous about this job of yours."

"Dat so?" Murphy cocked a brow as they stepped off the footpath to cross the street. He waved towards the one vehicle that slowed to let them pass. "She seems confident enough. Took me ages to convince her to give it a shot. And if things hadn't gone sour at the last pub, I doubt she'd be here at mine."

Refreshed by his honesty, Evelyn patted his arm. "I don't know about that. You were gaining ground. The only reason Piper stays in Galway is because of her Da and me. Though I've told her time and again she deserves her own life, she stays. I'm glad she's here. There's nothing for her in Galway."

"Except you," Murphy added.

"For now."

"You telling me you plan on leaving Galway?" Murphy asked.

"If Piper is to be in Castlebrook full time, then perhaps so shall I. It's time for both of us to realize we cannot compete for her father's affections. He has and will always choose his liquor over us."

"Which is a right shame. I've only just met you and believe I could pick you over a fine pint any day."

She chuckled as they emerged in front of Chloe and Layla's shop. "Well!" Evelyn gasped. "Isn't this just lovely?" Murphy opened the door for her, and she stepped inside to Conor McCarthy.

The redhead's forehead furrowed as he tried to decipher who Evelyn was and why she was on Murphy's arm. "Conor be part of the family as well," Murphy explained.

"Oh, another brother?" Evelyn asked.

Conor shook his head to the negative as Murphy said yes. Confusion flooded Evelyn's face.

Murphy grinned. "He's not blood, but he's most definitely a brother."

Conor's cheeks flushed at that as he extended a hand.

Chloe made her way back into the room using only one of her crutches, her other hand carrying a large glass vase. Conor jumped to attention and intercepted the vase and set it on her work table. She smiled in welcome. "I have some petals for you to look at right over here." She made her way towards a center pedestal that housed a small vase with a bright bouquet of dahlias.

"Oh how grand." Evelyn leaned over and sniffed. "Do they look like something Piper would like?" she asked Murphy.

Murphy shook his head and looked to his sister. "You have any of those pretty petals you ordered for Rhea's wedding? The pale pink ones?"

Chloe snapped her fingers on a nod. "I do. Hold on a second. Conor, would ye mind?" She motioned to one of her coolers and Conor opened the door. She pulled out a small black bucket. "These the ones, brother?"

"Aye. Those. That's what Piper needs, I think." He looked to her grandmother for approval. Evelyn beamed as she ran a finger over the thick blossoms. "Those are stunning."

"Peonies," Chloe told them. "Rhea's crazy about them. Had to order these specifically for the wedding."

"Oh, well I don't want to take from that." Evelyn told her.

"Oh no, ma'am," Chloe assured her. "These be extras. I loved them so much myself, I ordered a bounty. Will only take a minute to clip a few for you."

"That would be grand, Chloe," Murphy told her. He turned to Conor. "This be Nan."

Conor's eyes lit up and he heartily shook Nan's hand again. "Oh, well it be nice to meet you, for certain. We've taken a likin' to your Piper. Poor lass." His hearty laugh had Evelyn smiling. "Especially since she has to put up with this eejit most of the time." He thumbed towards Murphy and Murphy playfully narrowed his eyes before landing a small punch on Conor's arm.

"He's only brave enough to say those things while I'm injured," Murphy told her. "Because he knows I can't take him down."

Conor beamed and nodded.

"Here we go." Chloe rested her hands on her work table as the voluptuous blossoms were clipped short and placed in a small glass vase.

Evelyn reached for her purse and Murphy stilled her hand as he fished out his wallet. "Allow me." He handed Chloe more than enough money to cover the cost, but his sister stayed silent. Evelyn picked up the vase and surveyed it from all angles. "They are beautiful, Chloe, thank you."

"Very welcome."

"And this side of your shop, is there anything over here that Piper might fancy?"

"That be a question for my sister, Layla. That's her shop there. She would know what scents Piper favors. I can give her a ring if you like?"

"Oh, no. That's alright, dearie. I'll just have an excuse to come back by another time." She smiled. "I think we are all set then." She looked to Murphy. "I've stolen him away for the afternoon to be my guide."

"Good. He needs to escape the pub every now and then," Conor told her.

"Unfortunately, that's now where I'm taking him. On our way to Piper now."

"If you fancy a pint in a bit, ring me," Murphy told his friend.

Conor waved him onward as he and Evelyn walked the few paces towards the pub entrance. In the late afternoon hours and early evening, the music sat at a lower level than for the prime hours of the pub. He noticed a few regulars when he walked inside and offered waves in greeting. Piper was not behind the bar. The door to the back room swung open as Piper headed out hoisting a heavy wooden crate laden with bottles. She immediately set to work restocking the ice bins.

Murphy walked Evelyn forward and Piper briefly glanced up and then back to her work. When realization hit, her eyes darted back up.

"Nan!" She ran, ducking under the bar door, and popped up right next to them and embraced Evelyn in a tight hug. She turned her face away, but not before Murphy saw a lone tear slide down her cheek. "I see you've already met the town ruffian," Piper teased.

Evelyn swatted her playfully. "He's been nothing but charming."

"I'm sure he has." Piper nudged Murphy's good arm. "'Tis his way."

Evelyn's eyes danced as she watched the two stare at one another. It was obvious something lurked beneath the surface of their working relationship. But, as she watched them awkwardly take a cautious step apart, she realized neither of them realized it. Or if they did, they ignored it. The thought brought sheer joy to her heart. "You're earlier than expected," Piper told her.

"Riley finished up early and wished to meet up with his girlfriend, Heidi. I was all set, so it didn't seem like a bad idea to just leave early with him."

"I'm glad you did. Though I won't be finished up here for quite some time. Perhaps Murphy can take you by the bed and breakfast so you can get settled. Meet Sidna, Senior, and Roland."

"I've met Roland," Evelyn stated. "Nice man."

"He is," Piper agreed.

Evelyn held out the flower bouquet. "These are for you."

Piper took the vase. "Nan, you shouldn't have. They're lovely, but the cost—"

"Was worth it. They're beautiful," Evelyn interrupted her.

"But Da—" Piper's eyes pained as she looked up.

"Is not going to see any more money from either of us. 'Tis a new chapter you have here, Piper. A fresh start."

"But—"

"But nothing," Murphy interjected. "They be pretty petals, given with love. The perfect gift." He gently rested his free hand on Evelyn's back in acknowledgment. "And I can't think of anything better than for the two of you to share the rest of the afternoon and evening together."

"And who'd be manning the kegs?"

"Me. I am capable of running me own pub," Murphy told her.

"With one arm?"

"Aye. I bet I can manage just fine this once. Doesn't seem too crazy in here."

"It's still early," Piper challenged.

Sighing, Murphy walked towards the door and flipped the sign. Evelyn's eyes widened.

"Murphy," Piper stalked towards him. "I'm to work. You can't close the bar. People will be expecting their after-work drinks."

"And they can go elsewhere. I'd like you to spend time with yer Nan. Introduce her around. Eat at the family meal."

"Then you will too." Piper placed her hands on her hips.

"Fine. I will," Murphy replied. "But for now, you go on. I've things to see to any way."

"If it's the order for Rhea and Clary's wedding, I've seen to it," Piper told him.

Murphy ran his hand through his hair disappointed in himself for forgetting that order. It wasn't what he was thinking about, but he was thankful Piper did indeed remember it. "Aye."

"So, see... nothing for you to do now either. You might as well come with us."

"No."

"Murphy—"

"I'm bloody tired, Piper." His temper shot for a split second before having to admit he wasn't feeling that well. If he were honest, it was just over the last few minutes that he started to feel weak.

Sympathy washed over the women's faces. "I shouldn't have had you walk all this way," Evelyn fretted.

Murphy held up his hand. "'Tis not the walk that's done me in, Evelyn. I've had a busy day."

"Rest it is, then." Piper rested a hand on his arm. "Ice and rest. I can bring you a plate from your mam's. Don't even worry about coming to the family meal. Rest."

"I'm not an invalid." Murphy's argumentative tone had lost its edge and he started to feel himself growing more pitiful by the second. Which was easy to do with two females hovering over him so tenderly.

"I know." Piper began nudging him towards the back of the pub, Evelyn following. "I'll close out the pub. You go rest." She opened the door that led to his private quarters and all but shoved him through it. Murphy turned and met two pairs of steely blue eyes.

He smirked. "You two are quite formidable." He winked at Evelyn as he tugged a strand of Piper's silky hair, a habit he enjoyed. She swatted his hand away and nudged him again. "I hope you like yer flowers."

"I do. Now, rest. Ring me later if you feel up for company. I'll let you know if everyone's still at the B&B."

"Aye. I will. Have a care, ladies."

Piper took a step back into the pub. Their eyes lingering on one another a moment longer before he closed the door.

«CHAPTER EIGHT»

Nan had settled in at Sidna's B&B. She and Sidna clicked from the moment Evelyn's eyes fell upon the spacious kitchen. Piper knew she could now find her grandmother in that very kitchen, allowing Sidna to boss her around so as to lend a helping hand with the cooking for the café. Nan seemed happy and relaxed, a sight Piper hadn't seen in quite some time. She hadn't expected her to stay as long as she had but was glad that Nan felt comfortable in Castlebrook. They stayed up late talking about life and of course, Piper's father, but neither of them weighted themselves down with worry. At least, not in front of one another. Piper was surprised he hadn't found them as of yet or ventured down to hound them. *All in good time*, she thought with disappointment. But disappointments were to be shelved for the time being. There was no room for them with Rhea and Clary's wedding approaching at the end of the week. The O'Rifcan family worked 'round the clock to make sure everything was ready. Layla especially. Piper looked up from the bar as Layla waltzed inside, annoyance lacing her tone as she barked into her phone. "I can't, Delaney. I'm completely swamped. This wedding has me in fits. I will not rest or take time to rest until the last petal falls." Her face softened. "Aye, I miss you too. But I will be seeing you at the end of the week at the wedding and I'll be dressed in a pretty dress that you will compliment all evening." She giggled into the phone. "Oh, aye. And I you." She hung up. "For once I am the one too busy to meet up." Layla grinned. "And Delaney grows more pitiful by the minute. I rather like it."

"'Tis the power." Piper chuckled. "Careful there. For his heart is fragile."

Layla laughed. "Aye, I suppose so. I have been quite busy the last few days. Perhaps I'll surprise him tonight."

"I think you should. For both your sakes. Now, what brings you to the pub?"

"I haven't tracked Murphy down and I'm to pick up the wines for the reception. I'm taking them all to Clary's so that everything is already there for when we start setting up on Friday."

"Ah. Well, I have them in back. Want me to fetch them now? Or I could drop them by Clary's a bit later."

"Oh, that would be grand. Saves me the trip. I'm to hound Chloe about the flowers. She has but three days to finish all bouquets and she is just starting. I mean, I know she is a professional, but three days when she's still a bit slower moving than usual?"

Piper laughed. "I think she'll be done before you know it."

"I hope so."

"How's the bride?"

"Nervous, but excited. She and Clary can barely stand to be apart. She's taken the whole week off work so as to see to wedding details, and most of that time has been spent with Clary. Jeanie has been of wonderful help though, so I cannot complain too much."

"Well, just let me know what I can do."

"Aye. I will. Thanks for taking the bottles." Layla waved over her shoulder as she headed for the door, fingers already dialing the next person she needed to speak to.

Piper shook her head and sighed.

"The wedding of the century, it would seem." Murphy's voice snuck up behind her.

Turning, she cocked her head. "And where were you hiding?"

Guilt washed over his face. "In back. I wished to stand free of the tornado for a bit."

"Hm." Piper smirked. "Smart."

"Aye. I like to think so."

"I plan to take the crates over to Claron's here in a bit. Wish to ride along?"

"Aye. I would. I'll load them up now."

"Say again?" She eyed his sling and then rolled her eyes. "Don't you dare take that off, Murphy O'Rifcan."

He pointed to the door of the pub. "You see to closing us down and I will see to the crates."

Piper mumbled under her breath as she watched him disappear into the back room. She walked to the door and flipped the sign. It was just barely afternoon, but due to the wedding preparations for the week, Murphy had decided to only have the doors open the first half of the day. Business was slow during the morning hours, so Piper had spent most of the last few days polishing the wood furniture and scrubbing any surface she could get her hands on. Tables, chairs, and the bar now gleamed from her elbow grease. She heard a loud crash in the back room and sprinted towards the sound.

When she burst through the door, Murphy leaned against the wall, pain etched on his face as he held his arm and sling close to his chest. He took deep breaths though she could see a vein that appeared in his temple showing how hard he was biting back a scream. "I don't want to hear it," he growled through gritted teeth. He blinked several times and Piper stepped forward seconds before he fainted. She caught him as he slumped forward. Careful not to hurt his arm further, she supported his weight a moment before easing him slowly to the floor. His head lolled to the side and she lightly tapped his cheek. He didn't respond. Feeling a slight twitch of panic work its way up her spine, Piper searched her pockets only to find she'd left her phone in the other room. She fished in Murphy's pockets and found no phone as well. "Murphy O'Rifcan." She murmured in woe, resting his head in her lap. "You stubborn fool, open yer eyes." She slapped his cheek a bit harder. His lashes fluttered before his blue eyes looked up at her. Pain and confusion warred within them as he began to stir. "Careful now, lad. Easy does it." She helped him to a sitting position against the wall. He leaned his head back against the stones and inhaled a deep breath. "You alright now, love?" Piper asked, resting a hand on his leg.

"No."

His simple response had her lips tilting into a sympathetic smile. "You mustn't rush things, Murphy. I know you wish to help and go about like normal, but you can't. Not yet." Her voice was sweet and calm, in hopes that she might finally get through to him. She saw him eye the broken glass. He hadn't dropped any wine bottles, that was good. He'd only tried to lift a crate of glasses.

"I bloody hate this," he muttered. "Can't do anything to help with Clary's big day, and all because I was a right fool."

She smirked. "Don't be so hard on yourself. I do stupid things all the time."

Murphy scoffed. "Right."

"'Oh, I know it is hard to believe, but 'tis true. We all have our stupid moments, Murphy."

"And what, pray tell, are yer stupid moments? Because I have yet to witness one."

Piper's sarcastic grunt and sigh had him eying her closely. "Two words. My father."

She saw her words made Murphy feel even worse instead of helping.

"You're not stupid for wanting to help your father, Piper. It's admirable, really. Though I'm happy you and Nan have found peace here in Castlebrook this week."

"Aye. Me too. But the next time the Garda calls me about him, I know I will still help him, and that is why I feel stupid at times. At least yours was just a dumb cow." She couldn't help herself and a snicker slipped through.

"A bloody big cow," Murphy pointed out, but his lips tilted into his usual charming smile. She could melt into that smile, she realized, and the thought had her leaning forward and lightly brushing her lips against his cheek.

The movement caught Murphy off guard, and he turned in wonder. "What was that for?"

"For being kind," Piper explained. "And stupid."

"Well, if that's what I get for it, remind me to be so again." He leaned towards her, challenge in his eyes as he looked briefly down at her lips and then back up. "Piper?" he asked.

"Aye?" She felt her pulse jump at the sound of her name and wondered what he could possibly want to say to her after eying her the way he was.

"I've a notion to kiss you right now." His fingers twiddled with the hair that brushed her jawline, and her heart skipped.

"Oh?" Her voice cracked on the word as he leaned closer to her. She didn't move. She couldn't move even if she wanted to. His lips softly pressed to hers, testing, barely moving, as if he was registering whether or not his action was welcome. When she responded, he leaned in closer, cupping her cheek in his hand and tugging her towards him. *The man could kiss*, she thought on a contented sigh. She felt the effects of his kiss drift slowly from her lips to her chest, where the flutters rested comfortably beneath her racing heart. His mouth hastened, his fingers now behind her neck as he held her to him. When he slowly pulled away, his eyes poured into hers. She rested a hand against his chest and felt the pounding of his own heart and felt a wee bit of satisfaction in that. He released his hold on her and slid his hand to the one upon his chest. He squeezed her hand and kissed her palm.

"I've a mind to do it again," he admitted on a shy chuckle. "I've wanted to do that for quite some time, actually."

"Why haven't you?" Piper asked, her voice quiet in the large room as if they could be overheard.

"I wished to have you here for the pub and I was afraid if... if you sensed it was just for me fancying you then you wouldn't come. I thought I could keep you at a distance. Me arm situation seemed like a right work of Providence when you agreed to stay on. I wouldn't have to be near you all day."

"Gee, thanks."

He swallowed. "I meant I couldn't trust myself around you. I was afraid I'd let my feelings slip if I had to be next to you behind the bar all day. I needed time. Time, I thought, to get what I thought were frivolous feelings out of the way."

"But?" she asked.

"But 'tis impossible. Because I do fancy you. Quite a lot, actually."

"You're not half bad yourself."

He smirked and tugged on her hair. "Dat so?"

"You could be better looking, but..."

He burst into laughter making her smile as she shrugged. "Here." She stood and extended a hand. "We've a mess to clean up."

He groaned as he rose to his feet and she handed him a dust pan. "I'll sweep, you collect," she ordered. And they worked in silence as both of them replayed the kiss on repeat in their minds.

Murphy finally broke the quiet. "Do you really think I could be better looking?"

Piper erupted into hysterical laughter. "Worried now, are you?"

Murphy looked genuinely perplexed.

"Murphy O'Rifcan, you're a right many things, but ugly is not one of them." Relief washed over his face and she found it quite endearing that the most confident man she'd ever met still had a soft side. She walked towards him and grabbed his chin. She stood on her tip toes and gently tugged his face down towards hers and planted a sweet, brief kiss on his lips for further affirmation.

∞

The drive to Claron's was quiet. *Not awkwardly so*, Murphy thought, just silent. He wondered if Piper regretted what happened in the store room. *He* didn't, of that he was certain. When they pulled up in front of the cottage, Chloe, Conor, and Claron were standing at the edge of Angel's Gap as Conor hoisted the top portion of the arch in place. Claron held the other end aloft, waiting for Conor to finish placing the first.

"'Twould be an awful time for a tickle." Murphy wriggled his fingers as Claron stood with his arms above his head.

"Don't you dare," Claron chuckled.

Murphy stood and watched as Conor drilled and anchored the first beam into place.

"And how do you plan on decorating this, little one?" Murphy asked Chloe.

She grinned. "I've already started. I'm creating vines of blooms and will drape, filling in where need be. Simple."

Murphy considered her idea and nodded in approval.

"It's going to be beautiful," Piper encouraged. "Layla wished for us to bring the drinks. Where would you like us to put them?" she asked Claron.

"Give us just a second, lass." Conor looked down at her as he climbed down the ladder and moved it towards Claron. "We'll be about done in just a minute and can help."

Relieving Claron of his burden, Conor hoisted the second beam in place and anchored it. Claron dropped his arms and shook them. "I believe I've lost all feeling in me arms." He grinned. "Come, I'll help you unload." He walked towards Murphy's truck and lowered the tailgate.

"Declan will bring the kegs tomorrow. He and Tommy," Murphy told him.

Piper's brow rose. "When did this come about?"

"I sent them a text just now. I can't lift them with me arm in a sling, and they're a bit heavy for you to lift, so it made sense to make other arrangements."

"Aye. Agreed." Piper looked to Claron and smiled. "You ready for the big day, Claron?"

"As I'll ever be. At this point I'd be fine if we just said 'I do' at the B&B and have a meal afterwards, but Rhea would not have it."

"I don't blame her," Murphy laughed. "She wishes to marry her prince in a magical spot."

"Magical?" Piper asked.

"Oh, aye." Murphy bounced his brows. "This be the very spot fairies are born, Piper love. Magic at every turn. 'Tis the perfect spot for a wedding."

"I see." Piper patted Claron on the shoulder as she walked towards Chloe, the two women carrying on their own conversation as Claron and Conor walked back towards the truck with Murphy to unload the second load of crates.

"Not going to lie, the closer the time comes, the more nervous I get," Claron admitted. "It doesn't seem real."

Murphy surveyed his younger brother and noted the genuine concern behind his green eyes. "What doesn't seem real, brother?"

"I'm just afraid she's going to back out."

Murphy laughed at the absurdity, but Claron's serious face had him sobering. "Honestly? You're worried Rhea will change her mind? Are you a complete eejit?"

Stress and irritation warred over Claron's face at his brother's reaction. "Aye, very much so. What happens if life here in Castlebrook isn't what she imagines? She'll be leaving the city and having to commute. Life on the farm is a wee different than life in Limerick. She's leaving her country, her family... I'm just afraid she'll regret her decision, or when she starts thinking about it, decides it's not the life she wants and doesn't go through with the wedding."

"You have such little faith in our Rhea?"

"Excuse me?" Claron asked.

"You obviously seem to take darling Rhea for a frivolous female, which I assure you, she is not."

"I never said such a thing," Claron defended.

"That's what you're implying," Murphy explained. "I guarantee our sweet little Rhea has waged every angle and aspect of moving to Castlebrook. I'm sure her heart took even longer to convince due to what she went through with Oliver, and still she has chosen to marry you. I'd say she's thought it out a great deal. Do not doubt her, brother."

Claron ran a hand through his hair. "I don't doubt her love."

"Then you doubt your own?" Murphy asked.

"No. Of course not."

"Then what the bloody Martha are we talkin' about?"

"It's just—" Claron looked around to make sure no one else heard him. "It's me, Murphy. What do I have to offer Rhea *but* my love? We will never have a grand life of dinner parties and socials. I mean, I will strive me best to provide a beautiful home and life for her, but I'm afraid life with me is not... well, it's not glamorous."

"And you think Rhea wants glamorous?"

Claron shrugged. "It's one of me fears."

"Seems you've got all kinds of unwarranted fears," Murphy pointed out. "All equally ridiculous. Rhea loves you, Clary. And you love her. 'Tis obvious to anyone who sees the two of you together. Why, I'd count myself the richest man in the world if I find a love like the two of you share. You've no reason to fret. Rhea will not back out. She won't tear your heart out like Amelia. She won't leave you. She *loves* you, brother. Truly, inescapably, loves you."

A small smile tugged at the corner of Claron's lips as he rubbed the back of his neck. "Are we really that obvious?"

Murphy rolled his eyes in mock annoyance. "Are you kidding me? Every time I see the two of you casting glad eyes at one another I want to scream."

Claron laughed. "Aye. I do love looking at her. Not sure I'll ever tire of that."

"She's a nice one to look at," Murphy agreed.

"Thanks, brother." Murphy reached out and Claron gave him a firm hug both slapping one another on the back as they stepped apart. "I'm just letting me nerves get the best of me. Bloody devils."

"I can only imagine. There's still much to do and everyone's rushing around makin' you crazy. Good thing there's only a few more days," Murphy told him. "But guess what?"

"What's that?"

"Then you get to whisk your lass off to a tropical paradise for a relaxing... well, maybe relaxing..." Murphy winked. "honeymoon. And none of this will be here when you return." He waved a hand at the arch. "Because all yer little fairies will have seen to it that it's ready for you when you come home. That is, if we can convince Riley to hold off on his remodel plans until you get back."

"He better. I've talked with him about that. 'Tis my wish to cross the cottage threshold with Rhea the way it is before demolishing it. I think it is important to cherish the tradition of Grandda and Nan's legacy before we completely gut the place."

"So at least two days after your return then?" Murphy teased.

Claron grinned. "If Riley has his way, yes. I'm hoping I can convince Conor to have him start work on the McCarthy family home first." Claron nodded across the field and fence towards their friend's family property. "That would buy Rhea and me some time to settle in before demolition begins. But Conor is hard to sell on the idea."

Conor looked up from the porch and grinned. Not knowing what was said, but hearing his name, he stood. "Talking out the back of yer heads about me?" he asked as he walked towards them.

Claron pointed to the house across the meadow. "Talking about how you need to get that project started."

Conor sighed. "Aye, I know it. Sooner than later." He eyed Chloe with eyes full of longing as he watched her wave her arms through the air explaining to Piper her plans for the reception decorations.

Murphy and Claron shared a grin at their besotted friend. "And what of you, Murphy?" Conor asked, nodding a head towards Piper.

"What about me?" he asked.

"Any *plans* for the future?"

Murphy's face must have given away his earlier activities because Claron's brows rose in surprise. "No way? Really?"

"What?"

Conor hooted in laughter.

"You and Piper?" Claron asked.

"I didn't say anything," Murphy quickly shared.

"You didn't have to." Claron laughed. "The sloppy grin did it for you. When?"

Sighing, Murphy rolled his eyes at his brother's prying. "Just a wee bit ago, but don't make a big deal of it all. The lass and I haven't had a chance to really discuss the matter."

"Another one bites the dust," Conor muttered, his and Claron's answering grins making Murphy fidget.

"'Twas just a kiss."

"And I'm a ballerina," Conor added. Claron burst into laughter and the women turned to see what the men were up to.

"Quiet now, lads," Murphy hissed. He forced a smile as Piper and Chloe walked up.

"What is so funny?" Chloe asked.

"Murphy." Claron nodded towards his brother.

"Oh?"

"Oh, aye, sister. I'll have to tell you all about it later." Claron winked at her.

"Or not," Murphy added and had the men biting back more laughs.

"Ready to head back to the pub?" Piper asked.

"Actually, I was thinking of heading on over to the B&B. Perhaps we should see what Nan and me mam are up to today."

"I'd like that. I haven't chatted with Nan since last night."

"It's settled then."

"If you two see my future wife, tell her I've want to see her," Claron mentioned.

"Of course, you do, Clary," Murphy hounded. "Right pitiful, you are." He winked as he opened the truck door for Piper. "Conor. Chloe. We'll be seeing you." He tossed a wave to his family and directed his truck towards Mam's.

«CHAPTER NINE»

When Piper and Murphy cleared the threshold of the kitchen, shock had them both standing rooted to the floor as their wide eyes soaked in the scene before them. Flour covered every surface, as pies rested on the small round table against the wall. Dozens of them. Biscuits, cakes, puddings, and crusts lined countertops, tables, and chairs. Sidna and Evelyn stood behind the island working in easy chatter as they prepped what looked like more pie crusts. Lorena, the oldest O'Rifcan sister, stood at the stove stirring a large pot that contained what smelled to Piper like fresh berries being cooked down for a filling.

"What have we here?" Murphy interrupted.

The women's heads snapped up as he headed their direction, a kiss on the cheek for all of them. "All of you taste a bit sweeter than usual." He stroked his chin. "What could possibly be the reason?" He stood in the midst of confectionary chaos with a pleased smirk on his face.

Sidna waved away his foolishness with a smug smile. "Rhea and Clary wished to have a plethora of desserts, so a plethora is what they shall have."

"I'd say so."

Piper gave her nan a kiss and slid onto one of the stools and faced them. Murphy followed suit.

"And what has the two of you out and about?" Evelyn asked, pleased to see them together and in comfortable companionship.

"We've delivered the wine to Clary's," Murphy reported. "And we wished to see what shenanigans you two were up to. And poor Evelyn, being roped into yer madness." He tsked his tongue but grinned at his mam.

"We are lucky Evie has such a hand with the doughs," Sidna complimented her new friend, the new nickname not going unnoticed by Piper or Murphy.

"Evie, is it now?" he asked. "I like it." He winked at Nan and Piper's jaw wished to drop when she saw her grandmother blush.

"Oh, aye," Sidna continued. "So, we have Lorena manning the stove for us. No business at the café today because everyone knows I'm busy prepping for Clary's big day." She sighed, her eyes briefly daydreaming off as she envisioned her son's wedding.

"Speaking of Clary's big day," Murphy interrupted. "Is his bride about? He wished to deliver a message."

"She left but a few minutes ago with hopes of spending the day with her parents and Roland. I don't look for them to return until the meal."

"Everything seems to be coming together," Piper acknowledged. "We just saw Chloe at the Gap and the arch is up."

"Oh wonderful." Sidna beamed. "Conor's been right busy on that, as of late. And our Chloe... poor little dearie, with that leg. But she is doing her absolute best."

"She seems to have it under control," Murphy assured her. "She wobbled a bit without her crutch but seemed to feel fine without it."

"I hope so," Sidna stated. "I know she wishes to walk the aisle free of the crutch. For photo's sake. What about you?" She nodded towards his sling.

"Aye. I will probably stow the sling on the day."

"No, you won't," Piper firmly corrected, spinning her stool to face him. "Do you need a reminder of what just happened at the pub?"

His lips quirked into a dopey smile before he could help it and he leaned towards her. "Not that I need a refresher, but if you're offerin—"

She shoved his face away with an embarrassed flush to her cheeks.

"And what happened at the pub?" Sidna asked, curious as to the awkwardness that settled around the two.

"We kissed," Murphy shared while Piper, at the same time, mentioned, "He tried to lift a crate." Her face blanched at his announcement and the two older women burst into pleased laughter at her mortified face. Lorena turned towards the stove to hide her smile. He playfully tugged on Piper's hair and she swatted his hand away. "Oh, come now, Piper, don't be playing hard to get," Murphy teased.

"I'm not. I just don't see why you're announcing it to the world when we both know it shouldn't have happened and 'twill not be happening again."

"It won't?" He looked genuinely displeased with the idea and his mother and Nan shared a genuine look of amusement.

"Of course not, you eejit. We work together."

"Aye. But I don't see how that's a hindrance."

Piper groaned. "We are not having this conversation here." She stood to her feet. "We've work to do. We should head back to the pub." Standing, she brushed away traces of flour on her hands.

"Been on the payroll a week and already bossing me around." Murphy cast pleading eyes towards the older women. "She always been this bossy, Nan?"

Piper shoved his good shoulder. "Stop it." She turned and pointed to Nan. "And don't answer that. We're leaving."

Grinning happily as she nudged him towards the door, he attempted to wave over his shoulder. "Have a care, ladies!" he called as Piper continued their path out of the B&B.

"It would seem we have another romance brewing," Lorena told her mother.

Sidna beamed at Nan. "I think it a right good fit, you?"

"I love the boy," Evelyn replied. "And Piper seems to hold him in high regard. But we've got... our problems." Having filled Sidna in on her son's alcohol and gambling habits, Sidna nodded in understanding.

"Nothing an O'Rifcan can't handle. Murphy especially. He's seen it all at the pub."

"Piper—" Evelyn paused on a sigh. "I'm afraid she's been so disappointed by her father. It's almost as if she punishes herself for his actions. She's rarely dated over the years, always working to ensure she can take care of me and her da. I'd love to see someone flip the tables on her and take care of her instead. She's missed a lot of joy in her life because of her father."

"And joy is what Murphy does best," Lorena added, her tender smile encouraging Evelyn.

"Then I hope he's patient, because it may take some time."

Sidna chuckled. "I think Murphy has his mind made up now." She held up a finger for them to quiet. They could hear voices carrying through the exterior wall of the building, an angry Piper hounding Murphy.

"And I can't believe you just blurted it out like that." Piper ran a hand through her hair.

"They asked. I was being honest."

"Perhaps you don't have to always be so bloody honest, Murphy O'Rifcan. Have you ever thought of that?"

"I thought women appreciated honesty." His brow rose. "Am I incorrect in my thinking?"

She growled. "Don't twist me words."

He smirked as he shrugged. "Yer words, not mine."

"You're the most frustrating man I believe I've ever met."

"I'm really quite simple." He slid his free hand into his pant pocket and rocked back and forth on his heels as if he were passing the day away with friends. It irked her. Why was she so twisted up about their kiss and he seemed totally fine with it? Did he not realize it would now make things awkward between them at the pub?

"You're an infuriating man."

"Now *that* I have been told quite often." He grinned proudly. "'Tis a gift."

"Wipe that smirk off yer face." Piper stalked towards the truck and yanked open her door.

"You've no idea what you're getting yourself into with me, Murphy. Best call this to a close before we lose friendship over it."

"I've no intention of losing you, Piper O'Beirne. I like you." He winked over the top of his truck before sliding into the driver seat. She huffed in annoyance as she did the same.

She stewed on the drive towards the pub, but when they pulled into the parking area, Murphy placed a restraining hand on her arm. "Stay in the truck." He nodded towards the door to the pub, the wood splintered along the jam from someone having kicked it in.

Piper gasped. "What? You're not going in there alone." She unbuckled her safety belt.

"Piper." Murphy turned serious blue eyes on her. "Call Declan." He handed her his cell phone.

"I will not. I'm coming with you."

"Piper." Murphy's voice hardened, as did his gaze. "Stay put." He slipped out of the truck and walked towards the open door of the pub. He nudged it open with his foot. She watched as he disappeared inside. She grabbed his phone and pulled up Declan's phone number. Before she could call the brother, Murphy stepped out of the pub and waved her towards him. She hopped out of the truck.

"Did you call him?"

"Not yet."

"Good." Murphy took his phone. "We'll hold off on that for now."

"Why? Did they trash the place? Is it fine?"

Murphy's eyes softened. "No. But they're still here."

"What?" Piper barreled past him. When she walked inside, her stomach dropped. Her father, sipping a glass of whiskey, sat at the bar. The half empty bottle and his glazed eyes told her he'd been there a while.

"Da?" she asked. "What are you doing here?" She walked closer to the man, her steps cautious. She felt Murphy's presence behind her but did not wish to see the look on his face, his realization that this was where she came from. That this was her family. This was why nothing could ever happen between them. No one in their right mind would ever wish to deal with the baggage she carried. Baggage in the form of a drunken father who turned up unannounced and vandalized their establishment.

"Nice set up you have here." Her father's voice was gravelly and deep, raw from years of drink and yelling.

"Da, I'll be asking you again, what are you doing here?"

Her father's eyes hardened as he looked at her over the top of his glass. They briefly washed over Murphy before settling back over his daughter. "I come home to find your nan gone, a note saying she was visiting you. She didn't say where, but it didn't take much snooping to see her notes about this place. You leave Galway. You leave me." He straightened in his seat and turned to face her. "You leave me sitting in a jail cell, rotting away like some common criminal. You don't even give a backwards glance."

"Not true," Piper told him. "I haven't left Galway. Yet."

Her father's brow rose. "Yet? So you plan to? You plan to leave me? To leave everything you've worked for?"

"I have nothing in Galway. Everything I worked for is gone because of you, Da." Piper's voice shook as she tried to contain her anger. "I lost me job because of your episode last week." She felt a sudden wash of shame that Murphy had to witness her father this way. That he could now see why her previous boss did not want to deal with these interruptions anymore.

"You lost yer job because you lack dedication. If you can't be dedicated to family, then what's work to you? Yer boss could see that. He was a smart man. Went on and on about you. How you'd taken the night off and spent it with your friends right under his bloody nose."

Piper cringed, knowing it hadn't been easy to sit with Rhea and the girls at her pub that night, knowing she should have been working. She'd talked to her boss about it, and he was fine with her taking the time. Encouraged it even. But the lack of pay and tips was always a sacrifice for Piper, because of the man sitting in front of her. He cost her more than her own happiness.

"You need to leave," Piper told him. "I'll cover the cost of what you've helped yourself to and the door." She motioned towards his empty glass and the broken door frame.

He reached for the bottle to begin pouring another glass. "I'm not finished yet."

She grabbed the bottle from his hand, and he bolted to his feet. She jumped at the action and before fear or anger could settle in, Murphy was in front of her.

"I think that was your last glass, Mr. O'Beirne." He pulled the bottle from the man's grasp and slid it down the bar. "How about we set you up in a nice comfortable room? You can sleep off your drink there and have a nice meal awaiting you when you wake up?"

Piper watched as her father's eyes turned hard at Murphy's interference. "I don't like you, boyo."

Murphy chuckled. "Not many people do. Comes with the territory. I'm the likable sort, I assure you, just not when I'm having to take the bottle away."

He reached to help her father steady himself on his feet and her father shoved his hand away. "I'm not moving."

"Da," Piper stepped forward, eyes pleading. "listen to Murphy, please. He's offering you a kindness."

"And I don't want it."

Piper went to speak, but Murphy held up his hand. "Piper, could you fetch the bottle?" She eyed him curiously and slowly walked to the end of the bar. Murphy sat on the stool next to her father. He reached over his shoulder and unclasped the sling. "Bloody thing gets tiring after a bit." He tossed it onto the counter. Piper saw the distrustful, yet slightly curious look her father cast Murphy's way.

Murphy leaned across the bar top and fetched himself a glass and poured each of them a helping of whiskey. Her father's lips tilted at the corner. "I'm Murphy O'Rifcan, by the way." Murphy waved his hand to encompass the room. "This is my pub."

"Daniel O'Beirne," Piper's father introduced himself, as he and Murphy clinked their glasses together.

When Murphy tossed back his whiskey with no complaint, Piper saw the respect in her father's eye at such a talent. She inwardly cringed that something so simple impressed the man but was still unsure what Murphy was actually doing. She watched as he poured himself another glass and topped off her father's. "I've had a mind to enjoy one of these all day," Murphy told him. "Me little brother be getting married at the end of the week and the whole family is busy and in an uproar over it."

Daniel grunted in means of understanding. Piper slid beneath the bar door and began straightening the mess her father had made. She noted several broken glasses on the floor and began sweeping, her ear tuned into their conversation.

"Piper love," Murphy looked up. "could you fetch me a mineral?"

Her brow rose as she reached under the counter and slid a carbonated soda across the bar. "Unfortunately," Murphy began. "I'm still on some pain meds for me arm, so I have to pace myself."

He opened the soda and took a long and satisfied sip. "That be almost just as good right about now."

Daniel studied him, but slowly sipped the rest of his whiskey. The bottle was next to Murphy and out of his reach, so he'd either need to ask for Murphy to top him off or sit with an empty glass. Piper wasn't sure what her father would choose. But to her surprise, Murphy grabbed the bottle and filled his glass again without even having been requested. *What was he doing?* she thought. He knew her father struggled with alcohol. Though he'd already consumed more than his share, she wasn't sure he needed any more.

Daniel sipped the whiskey slower this time. Savoring the amber liquid as Murphy continued sipping his soda. "What'd you do to yer arm?"

"Piper beat me," Murphy told him.

Piper gasped. "I did no such thing."

Murphy winked and then laughed as Daniel's face split into an amused smile. "She packs a mean punch."

"Aye, she does." Murphy chuckled. "But no, it wasn't our lovely Piper who got me this time, but a cow."

"A cow?" Daniel turned to him to hear more.

"Oh, aye." Murphy began regaling him with the tale of Claron's stag party and the infamous cow that wouldn't move. He was a natural storyteller, and Piper found herself grinning like a fool as he added his usual charm and humor to the story. Her father was riveted as well and burst into laughter at all the proper moments which only encouraged Murphy's elaboration. She hadn't even noticed when Murphy had retrieved them fresh drinks, only this time they were both drinking minerals instead of whiskey. Her father chugged back the sweetened soda without complaint, and Piper stood in wonder at Murphy's ability to both serve and converse without causing a stir. "So, your darling Piper agreed to help me out. I'm a wounded man and can't handle the kegs with one arm, so she's lending her expertise. I'm right lucky to have found her when I did."

"And good thing she was free of that stuffy pub in Galway," Daniel pointed out, as if taking credit for Murphy's good fortune.

"Aye, there is that. I've been after her for months to make the switch, but she didn't wish to leave Galway or you and Nan."

Piper saw Murphy's words wash over her father and his face sobered a moment. "She's a good lass, our Piper."

She felt the sting behind her eyes at his words. He'd never said kind words about her. Or to her, for that matter. She caught Murphy's gaze and he smiled softly at her as he continued his conversation with her da. "Aye, she is. A bit mouthy at times," Murphy admitted.

Daniel hooted in laughter again and nodded emphatically. "Always. That lass has always had a mouth on her. For such a little thing, she packs a mean tongue."

Murphy chuckled as Daniel began telling stories of Piper throughout the years. Some of when she had to handle him coming home late from the bars, some from him reading to her when she was a child, memories she hadn't realized he even possessed or cared about. "She's a good lass," Daniel repeated. "A good lass." His words trailed off as if he hadn't thought about his little girl in a long time. He slid his empty mineral can away from him.

"Another?" Murphy asked.

Daniel waved him off. "No thanks. I've a full head and belly."

"Ah." Murphy laughed as he knocked back the rest of his own soda and set the can down. "Come. Piper's family is always welcome to a place to stay. Unless you were wishing to head back to Galway tonight?"

Piper's eyes widened at such a statement and she turned to find Murphy holding up a hand towards her to not intervene as her father stood to his feet and attempted to balance himself. He was wobbly from the amount of whiskey he'd drunk, but he wasn't belligerent, and that was new. "No, no Galway for me tonight, I'm afraid."

"Ah, well good. I'd love to hear more about Piper then. She's not very talkative when it comes to herself, but she sure does have an opinion on everything else." Murphy winked at her as he led Daniel to his personal flat attached to the pub. When they disappeared down the small hall, she rested her palms against the countertop and took stabilizing breaths to calm her sad, but touched, heart. Murphy had expertly seen to her father as if he were his favorite patron at the pub. She glanced up as he walked back inside the pub. "He's sleeping on me sofa. We didn't quite make it to the bed, but I think he'll be comfortable enough until morning. We can take him to Mam's for a hot breakfast when he wakes."

She looked at him, tears sliding down her cheeks.

"Oh, come now, love." He took a step towards her and without another word, wrapped her in a comforting hug and let her cry.

«CHAPTER TEN»

"*I've a mind to go* on a vacation after this wedding." Layla pounded her pestle against the mortar with extra force as Heidi sat at the worktable resting her tired face in her palm and agreeing.

"Come now, it can't be that bad." Riley rubbed a comforting hand over Heidi's back.

"'Tis not bad," Layla continued. "Just a lot of work."

"That you volunteered for," Murphy pointed out.

"Aye, and I would again," Layla stated. "But Heidi and I have legged it all over the countryside to bring this wedding together."

"And 'twill be beautiful," Chloe encouraged, her hands tying the stems of another bouquet. Murphy reached down and snatched a tool. Supplies cluttered Chloe's countertop: clippers, ribbon-cutting scissors, floral tape, wire, thorn strippers, ribbon, boutonniere/corsage boxes, and flower food. His little sister meant business, and as her hands diligently moved from one completed bouquet to the next blooms in line, she never broke stride as his siblings continued to discuss Claron and Rhea's wedding.

"What is left to do, Layla?" Aine asked, sitting on Declan's right knee as he occupied one of the few chairs in the shop.

"Not much, really. Mam and Evelyn have the desserts underway and will be preparing the side dishes tomorrow. Mrs. McCarthy be seeing to the meats. Tomorrow I expect all of you to be on time for the rehearsal. No excuses." She looked up from her bath salts and made sure to make eye contact with each and every sibling. Her eyes lingered a moment longer on Jace. He held up his hands. "I'll be there."

"Your sense of punctuality has been a bit skewed as of late, brother," she accused.

"Well, no worries there now. I've stopped seeing the lass."

"Oh, sorry to hear that." Chloe looked up from her work with sympathy.

"It wasn't serious," Jace assured her and smiled to ease her mind.

"And Piper agreed to man the bar at the reception?" Jaron asked Murphy.

"She will oversee the bar, but she won't be working it," Murphy said. "She's a guest of the wedding. I want her to enjoy it as such."

"So who will be pouring drinks?"

"I've lined up a couple of barkeeps from Limerick who will do a fine job of it."

Jaron kicked Tommy's foot to wake him up. The red headed brother leaned back in his chair, arms crossed over his chest and eyes closed. "I'm awake," he muttered. "Just listening."

The door to the shop opened and had them all turning to see Lorena finally arriving. "Sorry. Mam's had me running in circles. What have I missed?"

"Layla wishes for a holiday after the wedding," Riley explained.

"Don't we all?" Lorena asked on a small chuckle, her eyes sparkled as she looked at all her younger siblings. "'Twill be grand. Everything is already lining up to be beautiful, and Clary will have a lovely nuptial. As he deserves."

"Speaking of…" Murphy held up a finger. "Amelia is not on the guest list, is she?"

"No," Layla said. "Rhea thought it kind to ask her so as to mend feelings, but I did not send the invitation."

"Layla—" Chloe's eyes bounced up from her work again in concern.

"Don't Layla me. Amelia would only cause problems or be a negative Nelly all night. I asked Clary what he wished to do, and he said he did not care. So, I simply held onto the invitation."

"She's not *that* bad," Jace defended and had all the siblings looking at him as if he were a sasquatch landing on the moon. "To me, anyway."

"To you," several of them said in unison.

"And all of you have your suits?" Layla asked, looking to her brothers.

"Aye," they all replied.

"Good. And Conor?" She looked to Chloe.

"Aye. Right smart looking in it too." Chloe beamed in pride as she wrapped the sticky floral tape around the small bouquet in her hands. The full peonies and delicate roses in soft hues of pink would look powder soft next to the bridesmaids' gowns, and ethereal against the scenery of Angel's Gap. She reached up and snatched the scissors Murphy fidgeted with in his hands and snipped the tape. Without comment, she handed them back to him knowing he needed something to keep his hands busy.

"Seems odd, doesn't it?" Murphy asked. "That our Clary be getting married."

"I always thought Tommy would make the walk before any of us," Jace commented, and had Tommy peeking out of one eye at his brother in curiosity. "You seem the marrying type."

"What's that mean?" Declan asked, pointing to his wife sitting on his lap.

Jace shrugged. "Tommy was always so serious, especially about his lasses through the years. Just seemed he'd be one of the first to take the plunge."

"You didn't think I would?" Declan tossed back. "I'm older than Tom. I've had but one serious relationship and it started and ended with Aine when I met her at nineteen. We married right away. We've two children and a third on the way. You would think—"

"You're plugged?" Murphy's brows rose in surprise as did the rest of his siblings' as they stared at the couple. Aine's face flushed and Declan's mouth dropped as he realized he'd let their secret slip.

"I believe the polite term is pregnant," Lorena corrected Murphy with a smile as she reached to embrace Aine. "Wonderful news."

"We don't wish for everyone to know yet. We don't want to take away from Clary's big day," Aine explained. "We originally planned to tell everyone after all the wedding excitement." She eyed her husband with an amused expression of annoyance as he kissed her on the nose. "So please, if you could keep it quiet until then."

Murphy held up his hand in pledge, followed by Riley.

"The two loudest mouths in the bunch are the first to pledge secrecy?" Jace laughed. "This should be interesting." He raised his own hand and winked at Aine.

Everyone agreed to Aine's wishes and her shoulders visibly relaxed.

"All the tables and chairs are set. Table settings will be placed the morning of, and flowers placed an hour before the ceremony." Layla continued on as everyone listened. "If you need something before the wedding and can't find me, look for

Grace. She has offered to carry some of the load on the big day."

"Darling Grace." Riley grinned. "She would wish for an excuse to come see us readying ourselves."

Laughing, Murphy nodded in agreement. "'Tis her crush on you, brother."

Riley blushed as he rolled his eyes and Heidi slipped her arm around his waist, lightly kissing his jaw. "He's dreamy. What woman wouldn't want a little of this?"

"Enough of that, Heidi. No sense in making us all sick to the stomach. Oh, so I hear you had a guest last night, brother." Layla looked at Murphy, her eyes narrowed. "He won't be a problem, will he?"

None of his other siblings knew of Piper's father making an appearance at his pub, and he wasn't sure how Layla found out about it, except maybe through his mam. "He'll be no bother."

"Promise?" Layla asked.

"You have me word." Murphy's hands tightened around the scissors at his sister's prying into Piper's personal business. Business he knew would come to light, but he hated the fact that he was the one to share it.

"What happened at the pub, Murphy?" Declan asked. "Seamus giving you fits again?"

"No. Seamus is the perfect picture of health and good lad," Murphy assured him. "'Piper's da has come for a visit."

"Ah." Declan's brow furrowed when he spotted Layla's nervous gaze. "Is he trouble?"

Sighing, Murphy looked heavenward for the right words. "He's a strong relationship with the bottle. He was a bit sore over Piper coming to Castlebrook and showed up to let his feelings be known. Nothing Piper and I can't handle."

"As Conor repairs the door to yer pub," Layla pointed out. "Barreled right through it looks like."

His brothers all awaited further explanation at that.

"Look," Murphy began. "He won't be trouble. Daniel and I have an understanding. I think. He just needs help. I'm willing to give it to him, so are Mam and Da. I've already looped them in on the situation. Evelyn and Piper are staying at the B&B and so I've also approached Roland about the man. He is going to be staying with him until we figure out everyone's next steps."

"'Twill be good for him then, staying with Roland," Jaron encouraged. "If any man can get through to a person, 'tis him."

"Exactly. But please, for the love of all things holy, don't say anything to Piper. She's having a go of it as it is," Murphy implored.

"We're here for her." Chloe lightly touched his arm and softly smiled.

"I know it, and so am I."

"You sure you want to face something like this?" Jace asked. "A lass with an alcoholic father is no walk in the park."

"Are you speaking from experience?" Riley asked.

Jace shook his head. "No, but Murphy's not exactly been the dating kind for some time and here he is taking on a lass with troubles. Just a bit dicey, if you ask me."

Murphy fumed. "I wasn't asking you, brother. And Piper be a strong woman who doesn't need my help to handle the man, she's done it her entire life. I just wish to help. And she's worth the trouble. All of it."

"Wow." Tommy leaned forward, amused and impressed at the turn of events. "She's gotten to you now, hasn't she?"

"What?" Murphy asked.

"Piper," Tommy continued. "Has she settled there then?" He pointed to Murphy's heart and all his siblings eyed him in equal fascination.

"So what if she has?" Defensive, Murphy set Chloe's scissors back on the counter and crossed his arms. "I've a right to care for a lass, don't I?"

Lorena waved a hand between the crowd. "Alright, we are off task. Yes, Murphy, you may care for anyone, and I personally think all of us love Piper and consider it a smart match."

"Well, we haven't gotten that far." Murphy's shoulders relaxed as he dropped his arms and stuffed his hands in his pockets. "I've yet to convince her as to the brilliance of it."

Riley hooted in laughter and slapped him on the back. "Playing hard to get, is she?"

Murphy acknowledged him with a quirked brow, but his lips tilted as Riley continued to laugh.

"She'll come around." Lorena smiled along with the rest of the O'Rifcans. "You boys have a way about you, all bloody charming."

"And another one bites the dust." Jace shook his head in dismay. "We're falling like a house of cards. First Clary, then Riley, then Layla, then

Chloe, and now you?" He spread his hands. "When will the madness end?"

"'Tis been a year for love." Lorena beamed proudly. "And all of you chose well."

"Agreed," Declan and Aine replied.

"I know I did," Layla grinned. "Delaney Hawkins had no choice but to fall for me. I didn't give him a choice in the matter. 'Twas bound to happen because I pulled out all my charms."

"Spoken like a true champion of the heart," Riley teased.

"Don't judge. Heidi did the same to you and you know it." A sloppy grin spread over his face as he looked down into Heidi's eyes.

"Aye... that she did." He held a hand to his heart. "And speaking of, I've a mind to take my lass for a nice bite to eat. Is this meeting over?"

"Unless anyone has anything else to say, it is. I just wanted us all to have a moment, like we did before Lorena and Declan's weddings. The last sibling meeting before another family member is added."

"Tradition," Murphy grinned. "I like it."

"But you are all free to go and check on your lasses. I've a mind to take a drive to Limerick and bother Delaney for a bit. Conor will be here to sweep Chloe away for a bite, I'm sure."

"For Clary and Rhea." Declan stood, Aine rising to her feet as well as Tommy rose to his feet. They all gathered in a circle, draping their arms over shoulders and around waists. "May their life together be full of blessing, charm, love, and babes."

"For Clary," they all stated and hugged one another until laughs and giggles erupted from the tight embraces.

∞

Sidna bustled around the now quiet kitchen as she swiped already sparkling counters and restocked her provisional drawers with flour and sugar. Piper sat, chin in hand, at the island and half watched as she tried to think through the next move with Murphy. With her father. And even with Nan.

"I find," Sidna began, "that when I'm to contemplate a great many things, a cup of tea helps." She brought over a quaint cup with saucer, a delicate floral design etched on the side. She filled it with the kettle and placed the tea diffuser inside. "Give it a minute or two. Stronger is better." She smiled as she poured one for herself. "You wish to talk to someone?"

Piper leaned back on the stool as she placed her hands around the cup and warmed her hands. "I'm not sure where to even start if I did."

"I find that the best place to start is where the heart is most conflicted."

"That might be a tie, I'm afraid."

Sidna pointed to the small table and she made her way to a seat as Piper moved as well. "Start with what has you so blue on the eve of a happily ever after."

Piper smiled thinking of Claron and Rhea and the bundle of nerves she saw earlier from the bride as her friend left to enjoy quality time with her parents in Adare for the day. "I want that."

Sidna's brows rose in question as she took a sip of her tea.

"A relationship like Claron and Rhea's. I want that in my life."

"As you should. 'Tis a beautiful thing."

"I just... Well, I'm not sure it's in the cards for me."

"Why ever not?" Sidna asked.

Piper looked to her as if the woman would have to be daft not to know why.

"Yer father has nothing to do with whom you give yer heart to, love."

"But the man I love will have to handle me da. And that is the problem I worry over. 'Tis not fair that a man should have that concern."

"If he loves you, he does not see it as a bother."

"And that's just it, isn't it?" Piper asked. "Murphy isn't bothered a'tall it seems. He treated Da as if he were an old friend and somehow had him eating out of the palm of his hand. He's found him a place to stay. He's given him a task for the wedding. Did you know he has me da helping the keggers? *Helping*?! The only deal is me da cannot partake in consumption. And he *agreed* to Murphy's plan. My fear is that he will not hold up his end of the bargain and ruin Claron and Rhea's big day. He's failed so many times, I have absolutely no faith in him. And what does that say of me as his daughter? Am I a terrible person for thinking so little of the man?" She ran her hands through her short hair and sighed, her blue eyes troubled.

Sidna reached across the table and held her hand. "Support is an important thing for someone in his situation, but you've every right to make him earn yours. In the meantime, if someone is willing to try and help him, let them. Murphy wants to help Daniel, yes, because he sees a man who needs it, but because Murphy wants to take part of that burden from your own shoulders. He cares for you, dearie. Now, I know you two have yet to discuss the ways of the heart, but even if he can only help you as a dear friend, he will. 'Tis Murphy's way. He's a kind lad. Always has been. And he's helped many a man defeat the urges of the bottle. My goodness, 'tis part of the reason he ended up with the pub in the first place."

"I'm sorry?" Piper asked. "What do you mean?"

"He hasn't told you?" Sidna asked in surprise. "Well, I'm not sure why I'm shocked by that. He doesn't share it often."

Piper waited patiently for Sidna to reach the point of her story.

"Mr. MacLochlainn owned that pub for years. 'Twas passed down from his own father to 'im. But Mac had an addiction to the bottle that grew and grew until he couldn't stand straight. That was when Murphy began working for the man. Mac had no kin of his own. The family line ended with him. He'd wasted his good years staring at the bottom of the bottle instead of finding a decent lass and settling down, you see."

"This sounds familiar," Piper mumbled.

Sidna smiled reassuringly. "Murphy was a young boyo, just barely of age to be drinking the black stuff much less serving it, but Mac needed help and no one else wished to do the job. Murphy spent much of his youth and early days taking care of Mac more than the pub, but the pub thrived. People came to respect Murphy for his work and friendliness. Even his care of the old man. When Mr. MacLochlainn passed, he left the pub to Murphy."

"He inherited the pub?" Piper asked.

"Aye. Mac's death was hard on Murphy. Towards the end of his days, Mac had come around. Giving up the drink and enjoying sitting in the pub and visiting with his patrons is what he did most days until his last. He was a good man underneath his burden. And I think Murphy sees that in yer da. I know you may have a hard time seeing beneath him because you're too close to the situation. Sometimes it's hardest for family to see the need, but someone from the outside looking in may be the perfect person to help. For you and for Daniel."

"I don't want Murphy to feel he has to help him. I know he thinks I'm cruel in just ignoring me da, but I'm fed up with his attempts. He's tried to give it up in the past, and he's failed every time."

"Then perhaps it is time you take a step back, lass. There's no shame in that. He's a grown man. Eventually he will have to make the decision for his own life. You and Evelyn have tried to make that decision for him, but it's his own, love. His own decision. And I know it hurts when he chooses the bottle over the both of you. And I'm not saying it won't happen again, but we must let him try. Let us see if Murphy and Roland can help him. Perhaps we will all be surprised."

"But the wedding?" Piper placed her forehead in her hand in dread.

"Clary's been apprised of the situation and he thought it a grand idea. He knows the risks."

"I could never live with myself if their special day was ruined because of me da."

"It won't be. Have a little faith, dearie. Murphy's a plan in motion. Let him unfold it. It's been a long time since a lass has turned a glad eye onto our Murphy. Oh, he's had his flirtations, but never one to let a lass in close. When I saw you two together the other day, I knew you were his choice. Whether or not the two of you make a go of it, is up to you, but I've a nose for such things." She tapped the side of her nose. "And his eye is on you. And if I'm not mistaken, yours is on him. As it should be. Because he's a brilliant match. I couldn't have planned that one better myself." She chuckled as Piper bit back a smile at her subtle meddling.

"You've given me much to think about, Sidna. I thank you for your hospitality with Nan. I fear she never wants to leave Castlebrook now."

"Perhaps she won't." Sidna winked. "I've a scent of another relationship brewing there as well."

Piper's brows rose in question.

"Have you been so blinded by your own heart you haven't seen the bud of love unfolding for yer Nan?"

"Apparently so." Piper chuckled. "You plan to tell me?"

"Oh, now 'tis not my place."

Piper guffawed in laughter at the woman. "Seems to me you don't quite give a care that it is your place or not. Who has stolen Nan's attention?"

"Our Roland," Sidna whispered and then covered the beaming smile beneath her hand. "I just know it." She winked.

Piper relaxed in her chair with a contented sigh. "She's a catch."

"As is he."

Shaking her head in bewilderment, Piper stood and walked her cup to the sink. "You've been full of great advice today. I think I should go find Murphy now and... I don't know... talk." Her eyes turned slightly dreamy and Sidna grinned.

"Aye, a good talking to for the boyo. On with ye now. I've important things to do." Sidna waved her out the back door of the kitchen and watched as the petite blonde directed her steps towards Murphy's Pub.

"Congratulations," Claron Senior's voice bellowed through the kitchen as he walked his empty coffee cup into the room for a refill. "Seems you've made another match."

Excited at the prospect, Sidna giggled. "Aye, it would seem I have."

He kissed her cheek in passing. "You're relentless, love." He turned at the door. "But I love ye for it." Winking, he continued on his way to the sitting room.

«CHAPTER ELEVEN»

Murphy was pouring his grandfather, Aodhán, and Roland full pints when she walked into the pub. He briefly glanced up and smiled in welcome. Piper ducked under the bar door, ignoring Roland's greeting as she grasped Murphy's face and planted a firm kiss on his lips. Surprised and a bit confused, Murphy took a cautious step back. His grandda grinned.

"Not that I'm complaining, but what was that for?" Murphy asked.

"For being kind."

"I'm always kind," Aodhán's thick accent had her turning in his direction. He wriggled his eyebrows.

"And this is?" she asked.

Murphy laughed. "That would be me grandda. Ignore his flirting, Piper. He's a heart for pretty faces."

Aodhán, not denying the comment, stood shakily to his feet as he extended his hand. He lifted Piper's hand to his lips. "A stunner, indeed. You didn't lie about that." He looked to Murphy in agreement. "Nice to meet you, lass."

"You as well." Her eyes carried about the room. "My da around?"

Murphy pointed towards his flat. "He's taking a rest for a bit."

Annoyance flashed over her face and Murphy held up his hands. "He's not passed out," he told her. "Just resting. Withdrawals are a serious side effect."

Piper pinched her nose as she tried to calm down her frustrations. Murphy pulled her hand down and rubbed a thumb over her knuckles. "'Tis a good sign, Piper. Don't be frustrated. We're seeing to him."

"And gladly so," Roland assured her. "A fine man."

Doubtful, Piper forced a polite smile of thanks.

"Now, what are you doing here? I figured Layla had you spending the afternoon helping with last minute decorations."

"I've eluded her attempts," Piper said guiltily. "I... I wished to see you."

Murphy, pleased by that notion, nodded towards the back room. "Excuse us a minute, lads." He held the swinging door open for her to step through first and then followed. As soon as the door swung closed behind him, Piper's lips were on his once more. Her hands gripped the front of his shirt as she stood on her tiptoes. Murphy pulled her back a moment. "What has bloody gotten into you?"

Piper ran nervous hands through her hair. "I don't know. I've just... been thinking about you all day. And then your mam was talking to me, and I've been thinking of our kiss the other day. I just—"

He lifted her chin with his thumb, his eyes kind. "I've thought about it too. A bit too much to my liking, but 'tis the way of it, I guess."

Annoyance flickered over her face. "Well, if it's that disturbing, don't waste your time." Her temper flared and he laughed.

"I didn't say it was disturbing, just that it's haunted more of my thoughts as of late. Truth is, I like thinkin' of you, Piper." He slipped his arm around her waist and tugged her towards him. Her hand rested on his sling as she inhaled a sharp breath at their sudden closeness. "I just haven't quite thought out how I want to proceed."

"Oh." Disappointment washed over her face.

"I want to proceed," he amended quickly, kicking himself for making her feel like he didn't. "I just... I was hoping to make a more romantic gesture of it is all. Not in the backroom of me pub, with me arm in a sling."

She grinned. "And how would those two things change your gesture?"

He reached up and tucked her hair behind her ear. "For one, I'd have another free hand." He thumbed a finger over her bottom lip before kissing her. "And then I would have swept you away to a romantic spot under the stars."

"Oh really? You think I need romantic spots?"

"No, but I want to give them to you."

Touched, she draped her arms around his neck.

"I've a heart for you, Piper O'Beirne. And I wish to give you many a romantic moment. If you will have me, I promise to do just that."

Silence hung a moment. "Even with the baggage I carry?"

He brushed a fingertip down her cheek. "What baggage? All I see is family."

A soft sob escaped her lips as she hugged him. Everything felt right when she was in his arms and he fought back disappointment when she pulled away. "I don't know how you did it, Murphy O'Rifcan, but I think you've made me fall in love with you."

He beamed. "'Twas me charms."

"Blast yer charms," She told him. "'Twas your heart." She wrapped her arms around him again and he grunted. "Oh, aye, I've done bumped your elbow, haven't I?" Sympathetically, she rubbed a soothing hand over his sling.

"Barely a pain," he told her as he relished in kissing her once more.

∞

Hands clapped everyone to attention. "We are missing the veil," Layla's voice called out and all the women in the room began clucking about in search.

Piper spotted little Rose standing behind the floor length mirror and knelt down. She peered around the side and Claron's niece held a finger to her lips as she grinned. Rhea's veil rested haphazardly in her hair. "Looks good on you," Piper whispered. "But perhaps we should let Rhea wear it first, then you can have a go."

Rose nodded as she stepped out and Aine gasped at the wrinkled fabric. She removed it from Rose's head and handed it to Piper. Already scolding the small girl, Aine escorted her by the hand to sit on the cushion next to Aibreean. Layla swooped by and plucked the veil from Piper's hands and over to Grace who steamed the gowns hanging along the wall. Claron's cottage boasted feminine touches of wedding preparation on every surface and in every room as woman after woman readied herself.

Jeanie, Sidna, and Rhea were in the master bedroom, Rhea finally dressing into her gown. Grace handed Piper the veil. "To the bride," Grace ordered and motioned down the hall.

Piper knocked on the door and heard the resounding welcomes. She peeked inside and gasped at the sight of Rhea. Nerves tinged Rhea's smile, but she beamed as Piper stepped into the room. "A wondrous sight you are, Rhea." She held a hand over her chest.

"We are just testing the clasps and the bustle. I'm not keeping it on until it's go-time," Rhea explained.

"Claron's going to faint," Piper told her. "I almost did."

Laughing, Rhea looked to a picture of Claron and herself that he had on his nightstand and beamed. "I hope so. Well, not faint, but I hope he loves it."

"He will." Sidna squeezed her hand before wiping her own tears.

Jeanie began helping Rhea out of the dress and into her robe. The doorbell sounded and had the women looking at one another. "Rhea!" Layla's voice called down the hall.

Rhea walked out and towards the door, Piper and the other two women followed. Riley stood at the door with a single bloom in his hand. A rose of pure white. He bowed when he saw Rhea. "Darling Rhea," he began. "I bring you a gift from Clary."

Rhea bit back a smile as she listened. Her bridesmaids and Piper gathered around her.

Riley handed her the rose. "Since he is not allowed to see you today, he gives the kiss he wishes for via me." He winked as he kissed her cheek. "Oh, now, I like that." He pointed to the rose necklace around her neck. The one he'd gifted her. He flashed a quick smile towards Heidi as he walked away. Rhea had no sooner closed the door when the doorbell sounded again. Tommy fidgeted on the front step carrying her wedding shoes. He smiled at the sight of her. "Rhea," Not a fan of all the staring faces, he hurried through his words. "Clary wished for you to have a message." He turned the high heels towards her and Claron's handwriting was on the arches. Rhea eagerly took them from him and read Claron's sweet words. She reached out and hugged Tommy, planting a kiss on his embarrassed cheek. "Thank you." He made a quick exit and she shut the door.

"What do they say?" Chloe asked.

"I have no idea," Rhea said and giggled.

Chloe read the words. "Mo chuisle mo chroí."

"My pulse of my heart," Aibreean, Claron's grandmother, translated and had the young women turning towards her. "You are the pulse to his heart, dearie. Dat is what he says."

Rhea held a hand to her heart. "I think I need new shoes now. I don't want to mess these up." She laughed as Layla handed her a tissue and she dabbed her eyes.

The doorbell rang and all the women scurried over to see which brother was next in line. Jaron stood carrying one of Layla's glass bottles with a ribbon tied around it. "Lovely Rhea." He smiled. "I've brought you a little something, and though looks may be deceiving," He motioned towards Layla's bottle, "this is not on of Layla's potions. Clary made this for you." He opened the lid and wafted it under her nose and Rhea's brows rose in pleased surprise. "That's lovely."

"'He wanted you to always remember this day, so with the help of an expert," Jaron nodded towards Layla, "he's bottled your bouquet." Rhea looked at the lovely flower bouquets sitting in glass vases along Claron's counter and back to the bottle. Her hands shook when she accepted it. Jaron kissed her on the cheek. "Blessings, Rhea," he whispered, as he headed back from whence he came. She shut the door and waved a hand in front of her face to dry her eyes. "I can't take any more of these." Beaming, Piper took the bottle from her unsteady hands and laid it on the counter beside her shoes and Riley's rose. "I feel so foolish only giving him a love note and a handkerchief with our initials."

"Lovely gifts those are to him," Sidna reassured her as the doorbell rang again.

"I also think I will always love answering this door," Rhea joked as she swung it open to find Jace standing on the stoop. "I'm not much for words, Rhea," he began. "But it would seem that Clary is. My gift for you is this." He handed her a letter. "I hope you're good at following directions." He winked before leaning forward, kissing her cheek, and then walking away.

Rhea looked down. *Open on our one-year anniversary.*

"Talk about confidence," Heidi muttered and had Rhea laughing.

Rhea held the letter to her heart as the doorbell rang again. "Next man at that door gets a big sloppy kiss." Rhea laughed as she thumbed another tear aside. When Layla swung open the door, Declan stood holding a small, black box.

"Easy now, he's already married," Heidi whispered and had Aine laughing across the room.

Declan quirked a brow towards his wife as he extended the box towards Rhea. "You already bring such sparkle to Clary's life, but he wished to bedazzle you a bit more, Rhea dear." Rhea opened the box and a set of emerald earrings glistened up at her. "Clary knows that leaving the United States and making the Emerald Isle your new home is a big decision, and he is forever grateful that you've accepted your place here. He wished to give you emeralds of your own."

Rhea closed her eyes and just shook her head. "If he only knew how easy he made that decision for me. That man…"

"Lovely." Chloe peered over her shoulder at the jewels.

Declan leaned over and kissed Rhea's cheek before leaving.

Layla glanced at her watch. "Bloody Martha! We need to get dressed. Bride and bridal party are to have photos taken in an hour." She clapped her hands.

Piper wondered where Murphy was and why he had yet to make an appearance. Disappointment must have shown on her face because Chloe leaned over and whispered. "I'm sure he has his own gift for Rhea coming soon."

"Did I look that pitiful?" Piper laughed.

Chloe grinned. "We've all had that look at some point. I'm glad it is for Murphy." She hugged Piper briefly around the shoulders before limping towards the room in which her dress awaited her.

It didn't take long for Rhea to be dressed and ready for portraits. Her hair and makeup were touched up and her mother draped her veil in just the right way, as mothers know how to do on wedding days. Sidna clucked about the cottage, ordering people to empty glasses and remove any such concoction that might stain a white dress as they made their way to the front door. Layla held a walkie to her lips. "Bride is on the move. Groom best not be peeking."

Murphy's voice carried over the line. "Groom is hidden. Groomsmen are awaiting the bride. Over."

The doorbell rang. Layla growled. "Of all times for them to choose." She yanked open the door and a smiling Murphy held the walkie in his hands and slipped it into his pocket.

He peeked around his sister to an awaiting Rhea and held a hand to his heart. "Rhea darling." Rhea beamed but held her finger up in warning.

"Don't make me cry, Murphy O'Rifcan, or I will sic all these women on you for ruining my makeup."

He grinned and held out a shot of whiskey. "My gift from Clary. For the nerves." He winked and laughed as Rhea knocked it back. "Atta girl." He held out his arm. "I should like very much if you let me escort you to the photo session. I've never stood beside such beauty."

"And there it is…" Heidi slapped him upside the head as she passed them. "She's almost a married woman, Murphy. Mind yourself."

He chuckled as he turned and stole a quick perusal of Piper standing in the cottage doorway. "Hold that thought a moment, Rhea love. Give me just one second." He released her arm and sprinted up the stoop to the cottage, pulled Piper with his good arm into a crushing embrace and planted a mind-blowing kiss on her lips that had every woman in the vicinity weak in the knees. He released her and quickly darted back to Rhea's side as if nothing happened. "Shall we?"

Piper stood reeling, her mouth trying to find words but her heart tripping over what had just happened. She grinned like a love-sick fool as she watched the man she loved walk Rhea towards the arch.

∞

"Easy Clary," Riley warned. "Or you're going to wear a hole in the ground."

Claron paced back and forth as he waited for Grace to come and fetch them. It was almost time for the ceremony. Currently, his brothers escorted family and friends to their seats. Riley and Conor waited with him as Murphy awaited the cue from Grace. He wasn't able to escort guests due to his arm injury. He'd stowed the sling for the ceremony but aimed to slip it back on for the reception. He was in bloody agony but refused to let the pain show for such an event. He saw Grace wave his direction. He poked his head inside. "'Tis time, brother."

Claron straightened his jacket and ran a nervous hand through his hair. Riley quickly slapped the hand away and fixed the unruliness Claron had caused to his mane.

Conor gave him an encouraging slap on the back as they walked towards the arch.

"I think I'm going to be sick," Claron whispered and had them all three laughing. "In a good way."

"Hold it in, brother," Riley warned. "Nothing would ruin the moment than vomit."

"You think I'm kidding," Claron whispered. "Me stomach is tied up in knots. My heart is poundin'. I feel faint."

Murphy cast a worried glance towards Riley. Riley paused and turned, placing his hands on Claron's shoulders. "You love Rhea, right?"

"Of course I do."

"And you want to marry her?"

Annoyed with the self-explanatory questions, Claron replied, "Of that I have no doubt."

"Then man up, brother. 'Tis normal to feel nervous, but you'll regret giving into the nerves if you do."

"I'm not going to," Claron told himself as well as them. "Just so many people staring."

"People who love you," Conor told him. "and are happy for you."

"Aye. I know." Claron swallowed the lump in his throat. "Let's do this. I'm ready for Rhea to be my wife and I'm done wearing this suit."

"Easy now." Murphy grinned.

"I didn't mean it like that." Claron flushed. "Just meant I feel smothered by it. I'm ready to rid myself of the jacket."

"Whatever you say," Murphy teased as they all neared the arch's center. As soon as Claron took his place, the music started.

Glancing up, Murphy caught Piper's eye as she filled a spot beside her grandmother behind the row of family. He was glad they had her sitting near them. Touched even, that his mam would think of such a thing. Her father sat beside her, and despite a few shakes here and there, he was composed. Overcoming his addiction one day at a time with the help of family and friends. It was to be a long road to recovery, Murphy knew, but he was hopeful that with his help and those around him, Daniel would indeed make a full recovery. Not just for his sake, but for Piper's as well. Chloe limped her way down the aisle. Though her stride was interrupted by the bulky brace beneath her dress, she still moved with elegance and he saw the proud smile Conor held as he puffed out his chest. She stared at only him as she came closer and then her green eyes shot towards Claron with an encouraging smile.

Heidi was next and looked like a vision.

"Holy Martha," Riley muttered and held a hand to his heart, making Claron chuckle. "I feel for you, Clary, for they only keep getting more beautiful."

Layla walked the aisle and settled in place beside Heidi as the music changed. Jeanie stood to her feet giving Claron a warm smile before turning and waiting to see her daughter walk the aisle.

On one side of Rhea stood Roland and on the other her father, Paul. She looked a vision, Murphy thought, and he heard Claron's quick intake of breath as his brother took a slow step towards her, an imaginary pull tugging them closer and closer. Claron's feet moved of their own volition and Layla whispered for him to stay put, but no one's voice could have stopped him from walking towards Rhea. Blinded to everything surrounding them, Claron walked up to his bride mid-aisle and clasped her face in his hands. Rhea's eyes widened in surprise before she smiled. He kissed her heartily and had everyone cheering and laughing. When he released her, it was as if his trance was broken and he realized his folly. Scarlet crept up his neck as he took a cautious step back from her. Roland patted him on the shoulder and pointed towards his place by Riley and had the audience smothering their laughs. Embarrassed, but too happy to care, Claron hurried over to his spot and waved for them to continue their march.

Rhea beamed as her father brought her to a stop and kissed her cheek. Roland did the same, as they handed her into Claron's awaiting hands.

"I'm sorry about that," Claron whispered. "You're… captivating."

Rhea blushed as she squeezed his hand. "And you too."

The minister took his turn and walked them through the vows, each line a simple yet profound pledge to love and honor one another. Murphy watched as not a dry eye on the cliff was to be seen and the love shining from Rhea's gaze on his brother had his own knees wishing to melt. The two were a radiant sight. And as the sun drifted lower in the horizon, the pronouncement came.

"You may *now* kiss your bride," the minister announced on a laugh as Claron dipped Rhea in his arms and passionately planted a storybook kiss upon her lips. Everyone cheered as they righted themselves. "Mr. and Mrs. Claron O'Rifcan."

The band began a lively jig that had Claron and Rhea scurrying up the aisle in joy towards the cottage, where a first toast would be shared amongst the wedding party as they waited for their after-ceremony photo shoot and for the guests to make their way towards the reception area. Petals rained down around them as Murphy made his way up the aisle with his brothers. He extended his hand towards Piper along the way and she hesitantly took it. He pulled her to her feet and tugged her along with the rest of them. When they reached the cottage, Claron leaned backwards and let out a loud sigh of relief before he claimed Rhea for another kiss.

∞

"Da, just sit tight."

"I'm to help, that was the deal." Daniel's gruff voice shook as did his hands as he crashed into a free chair behind the bar area of the reception. Piper glanced around to make sure no one noticed. "You're in no condition to help at the moment. Murphy will understand."

"I can't do this, Piper." His terrified gaze met hers. "I know I've been a horrible father to you. I know it. I've come to realize how bad, and it makes me feel even worse knowing I can't beat this. I can't. I just need a little to take the shakes away. To take the edge off and then I can help."

"No," Piper told him. "You've been sober for four days now, Da. Four days. You're over half way to a week. And then from there we will work on two weeks. But you are not going to have a drink. Be strong."

Daniel shook his head. "My bloody head is killing me." Piper looked up to see a happy Murphy as he danced with Rhea, twirling her about the dance floor as others awaited a turn with the bride. He briefly caught her eye and his brow furrowed. She cringed. He knew something was up and here she was stealing the joy of the evening all because of her father. It was less than a minute later that Murphy was at her side.

"What seems to be the problem, Daniel?" Murphy asked, knowing full well what it was.

"He's... not doing well," Piper reported.

"Ah. You know what, it sounds like you need a bit of sustenance. I've just the lass to do that for you." Murphy helped Daniel to his feet and escorted him towards Conor's mother. Mrs. McCarthy scooped a heaping pile of food onto a plate and handed it to the man. Murphy helped him stabilize his plate as he walked him towards a table to eat. Roland and his grands sat around the table. "All work and no food can really get to a man," Murphy chatted, giving Roland a brief nod to look over Daniel. "Eat up. When you're feeling a bit better, you can start clearing some glasses." Daniel nodded as he took a bite.

Piper met Murphy half way and he pulled her onto the dance floor. "What are you doing?" she asked, Murphy expertly swiveling her away from her father's direction.

"He doesn't need you hoverin' when he's in such a state. Let him be," Murphy whispered. "and dance with me."

"But—"

"Piper," Murphy bent his head down so she'd look him in the eye. "Trust me, alright?"

She exhaled a deep breath to calm herself. "I trust you."

"Good. Now make me feel like the luckiest man in the world and plant one on me."

"A punch?"

"Haha." He smirked. "That would be quite memorable now wouldn't it? I was thinking more along the lines of something like that?" He pointed over her shoulder and turned her to see Conor giving Chloe a sweet kiss as they danced.

"Oh. I see." Piper gave him a brief kiss. "How's that?"

"A bit short," Murphy whined. "But I'll take it."

"Good." She chuckled as he twirled her in a circle and brought her back to his frame. "How's the arm?"

"Bloody killing me, thanks for asking." He laughed though she could tell he was telling her the truth.

"I wished to give you a spin before confining myself to the sling. Then I believe my brothers wish to have a turn with you."

"Oh? Any cute ones?" She peered over his shoulder and giggled as he poked her in the side.

"We're all cute."

"Now that is a very true statement," she agreed. "But I think I like you best."

"You better." He rested his forehead against hers. "Because I have no intention of letting you go, Piper O'Beirne. Never."

She rested her head against his chest, the strong steady drum of his heart beneath her ear. She breathed him in, his now familiar scent calming her nerves and washing away her fears. "I'd like that." Looking up into his crystal blue eyes, she smiled. "I'd like that very much, Murphy O'Rifcan."

«EPILOGUE»

Claron and Rhea

The pounding of hammers had just about driven her mad and as she eased to her swollen feet, Rhea heaved an annoyed sigh when it took her two attempts to pull herself up from the chair and to a standing position. She shuffled her way towards the living room and Riley looked down from the ladder as he hammered into a beam. "Rhea darling, you're looking fine this mornin'."

"I know you're lying but thank you. How much longer of this?" She motioned towards the mess of her freshly remodeled home.

"A few hours or so. Is it bothering you?"

"Yes," she admitted. "Though I know you're not meaning to. I think I will go to the B&B and visit your mother. Perhaps I'll be able to have some peace for a bit." She rested her hands on her swollen belly and Riley nudged his hammer under her chin to lift her eyes to his. "Everything alright?"

Her smile softened. "Yes, I feel fine. Just achy. My feet are killing me and I've only just now started walking about. I've been sitting all morning and I feel like a giant balloon. Claron's been gone all weekend to Cape Clear and won't be in until tonight, and— I'm whining, aren't I?"

Riley stepped down the ladder and hooked his hammer in his tool belt. "Aye, but you've every right, being as big as a house and all."

Rhea's mouth dropped. "Riley!" She swatted him as he laughed and pulled her into a hug. "You're a beautiful house, though, and I plan to have this one just as beautiful before that wee babe comes along. Go. Let Mammy fret over you a bit. Get some rest. I'll notify you when I'm out of your way."

"Thanks." Rhea reached for her purse and then sighed, frustrated that it was on the floor next to the door and she couldn't quite bend over to reach it. Riley laughed as he snatched it for her. "Sure you don't need a ride? Can you fit behind the wheel?"

"Not funny, Riley," she called over her shoulder as he watched her waddle towards her car.

Rhea felt sudden relief when she closed the car door and drowned out the sounds of Riley's hammering. As she made her way towards Sidna's, she felt the usual thankfulness of having such a family to call her own. Her parents would be flying into Ireland by the end of the week. Now that she was to take it easy, Rhea needed help around the newly enlarged cottage. It was also plenty big enough to house her parents since her grandpa, Roland, had eloped with Evelyn, Piper's grandmother, and they now lived in a larger flat in town. The original design of the cottage's remodel was to give Roland his own space, but instead, would now serve as a guest quarters for Rhea's parents when they came. Funny how that all worked out, and funny how her grandpa had found love again so late in life. And so quickly. She smiled at the thought of the two lovebirds, and her lips spread further when she spotted Evelyn— Evie, as she liked to be called— stepping out of the B&B when Rhea pulled to a stop. The woman hurried over and opened Rhea's door. "You are just more radiant by the day, Rhea dear," she complimented.

"I don't feel so radiant." Rhea accepted her hug and help up the sidewalk and towards the welcoming red door that changed her life less than a year ago. The familiar warmth filled her heart as she stepped inside.

"I'd stay, but your grandfather and I are meeting at McCarthy's Restaurant for a bite to eat."

"Have fun." Rhea waved as Evie, with a spring in her step, made her way up the sidewalk.

"If you forgot something, I'm to remind you, you're late," Sidna called out as she stepped into the sitting room wiping her hands on a dish towel. "Oh, Rhea dear. I thought you were Evie." Rhea rested her hands against her lower back. "Come dear, have a seat. You poor thing, I've a mind to call your doctor a liar if he says you still have two months until delivery. Why you look like you're to burst at any moment."

"I feel that way." Rhea eased onto the sofa. "I've come for a bit of peace and quiet. Riley's working on the house."

"Oh, that boyo. I told him to stay out of yer hair. He wants to finish so badly for you though."

"I know. And I'm thankful. I'm just sort of feeling sorry for myself right now. Missing Claron and wishing not to feel so..." She encompassed her stomach. "This."

Sidna chuckled. "Oh, I remember those days. Well, in fact. Here," She bustled over and propped Rhea's feet up on a couple of throw pillows. "rest. I'll make sure you are not bothered." Rhea hissed as she shifted. "Sorry, my back has been especially achy this morning. It's pinching. I guess the baby is resting on a nerve."

"Perhaps so." Sidna left Rhea to rest and grabbed the phone off the wall. She dialed. "Clary, 'tis your mammy." She paused as she heard his voice and background noises of roadways drift through the phone. "You best hurry yourself home. Rhea's time is near— Because I'm a mammy and I know the signs. Hurry."

∞

Not that he needed a call from his mam to tell him to hurry home— he'd been ready to see Rhea the moment he'd left— but Claron needed to swap some calves and cows with his grands. Part of the business. He was on the last stretch towards Castlebrook having left before light. He'd felt something in the air this morning that told him to come home. Though he and Rhea still had two months before the official due date, Rhea was about to burst and had even told him she felt she'd deliver early. Time would tell, he supposed. But he didn't want to be away from her any longer than necessary. Their decision to start a family right off seemed like a great plan until he saw the transformation in Rhea. The poor lass had tripled in size and looked like she could snap if she were to bear any more weight in the middle. She was beautiful carrying his babes. Yes, two babes at a time. He grinned to himself thinking of that little surprise. Though he and Rhea decided to keep that fact a secret from the rest of the family, they knew they'd be expecting twins. That fact was another reason Rhea's notion of delivering early wasn't so outlandish.

He pulled to a stop at the barn and went about unloading the cattle. He saw Riley and a work crew steadily putting the finishing touches upon the cottage. When he closed the gate, he sprinted up the hill towards home. Rugby greeted him, lolling tongue and happy jumps around his feet. Riley gave a wave in greeting as he climbed down from the ladder. "Your wife is at Mam's."

Claron ran a hand over his face as he caught his breath. "I'm headed that way."

Concern etched Riley's brow. "Something wrong?"

"What?" Claron turned. "No. Sorry, I'm just eager to see her with me own eyes."

Riley smiled. "She looks like she's about break. What did you do to her, brother?" He winked.

Claron just shook his head on a laugh as he sprinted back down the hill to his truck. Rugby followed faithfully and barked as he backed out of the drive and headed towards town. When he pulled behind Rhea's car, he darted towards the door. He barged into the B&B, his mam sitting by

Rhea and rubbing her lower back. Rhea looked up and relief flooded her gaze.

"I'm so glad you're here." She started to cry and he hurried towards her. Sidna moved out of the way as she fretted towards the kitchen. Claron kissed Rhea's forehead. "Are you in pain?" he asked.

"Yes, but I don't think it's labor. My back is just out of sorts I think." She pulled him towards her and claimed him in a slow and steady kiss. "I needed that."

He grinned. "Aye, me too. Let's have Aine come take a look at you. Perhaps she will give you some relief of sorts."

"Yes. If she's around, that would be fantastic."

Claron nodded towards his mam to make the call and she quickly did his bidding.

"Did you have a good—" She grimaced a moment and hissed. "Trip?"

Claron reached behind her and began massaging her lower back. She groaned. "I don't like this, Rhea love. This isn't normal. Is it?"

"How should I know?" she asked on forced laugh. "I've never had babies."

"Aye, I suppose not." He kissed her temple. "I'm sure glad you've chosen mine to have though."

"Don't be sweet to me right now, Claron. Inwardly I'm cursing you at the moment." Her face tightened again and she leaned forward.

"I'm sorry, love." He rubbed her back as the front door opened and Aine walked in carrying a medical bag.

"What's the matter?" Aine knelt in front of Rhea and began checking her vitals.

"Back pain. And cramps. Are these the Braxton Hicks contractions you were warning me about?"

Having had a baby a couple months prior, Aine was still on maternity leave from the hospital and had tried to fully educate Rhea on what to expect. Aine's face turned to pity. "No, I'm afraid not."

"So, this is just normal?" Claron asked.

"Aye, it is, I'm afraid. But you need to get her to the hospital. Rhea's in labor."

Claron fell into the closest chair as Rhea's face paled. "But it's early," they both said.

"But not abnormal, especially on a first pregnancy and... well, with your secret," she whispered to them and then held up two fingers. She'd figured out their predicament. "I'd hurry. If you have any wish of meds for the pain, you'd best get there."

Claron stood and reached for Rhea's hands. As she stood to her feet, she gasped. Claron felt it before he looked at his shoes. Rhea's water broke and ready or not they were about to become parents.

Riley and Heidi

Hanging up the phone, Riley looked to his crew. "Gotta go, lads. I'm to have a brand new niece or nephew here shortly." He beamed proudly as he unhooked his tool belt and tossed it on the nearest bench. "Clean up once you're done. There's to be a babe coming here in a few days." He waltzed out the door his fingers already dialing Heidi's number.

"Well, hi there, handsome. I was just thinking about you. Looks like I might have to cancel our dinner plans. Delaney's being a pain," Heidi answered and Delaney's annoyed voice flooded from the background.

"Your boss will have to be forgiving, lass, because the two of you will need to call it an early day."

"Why's that?" Heidi asked intrigued. "Because Rhea and Clary are headed to the hospital. We're about to have a babe."

Heidi gasped. "No way! That's so exciting! I'll grab my purse. We'll be there!" She squealed again and he held the phone away from his ear.

"Careful on the way, love. I can't lose me beautiful fiancé because she's driving like a lunatic."

"I will be. Love you. See you soon." She hung up and Riley wound his way through traffic towards

Shannon hospital. He hoped he made it in plenty of time. He factored in the time it would take for Rhea and Claron to arrive at the hospital and calculated that he'd arrive only ten minutes after them. Perhaps. Hopefully. His phone rang again and Layla's voice carried over the line. "I'm to ask you about the cottage," she began. "Mam informed me it needed a fresh cleaning today."

"Did she now?" he asked, surprised by the lack of enthusiasm on his sister's part.

"Aye. I feel like I just cleaned the place. Surely you and your men haven't made that much of a mess."

"Did Mam tell you why it needed to be cleaned?" Riley asked.

"Because it was needing it," Layla repeated annoyed.

Riley laughed. "When did she tell you this?"

"This morning. Why?"

Riley sighed. "Ah, that would explain it then."

"Explain the bloody what?" Layla asked impatiently.

"Why you aren't thrilled that Clary and Rhea are on their way to Shannon Hospital to have their babe."

"What?!" Layla's scream flooded through the line and he cringed much like he did with Heidi's.

"Aye. I'm headed there now. You best be on your way. Heidi and Delaney know and are headed there."

"Good. Oh, good. Oh, goodness, I need to clean their house!"

Laughing, Riley calmed her fears. "You've a few days yet. Rhea will be in the hospital for at least a couple days afterwards. Clean it then."

"You're right. Of course. Yes, I'm on me way. Does Chloe know?"

"Not sure."

"Calling her now. Thanks for the report, brother. Keep me informed until I get there."

"Aye. I will."

∞

"Come on, Delaney, you're killing me." Heidi waited at the elevator and tapped her toe impatiently as her boss sprinted to his office and hurried back with a gift bag.

"What is that?"

"For Rhea and the baby. I've had it for weeks."

Heidi's brow rose. "Always the prepared one, aren't you?"

"Well, have you seen her lately?"

"That's not nice, Delaney." Though she couldn't help but laugh at his bluntness.

"I mean, I didn't mean it to be rude. She just... looked like she could go into labor with the slightest sneeze. I wished to be prepared."

"Right. Well, I'm driving, otherwise we'll never get there." She mimicked a slow driver, by moving her hands in slow motion as if she were setting a car in drive and shifting the gears.

"Very funny. I'm cautious. There's a difference."

They rushed to Heidi's sports car and hopped inside, the engine firing up. Delaney had yet to buckle his seat belt and Heidi was already blazing out of the parking lot. "I'd like to bloody make it in one piece, mind you."

"You will. And in record time." Heidi beamed as her cell phone jingled. Before she could remove her hands from the wheel, Delaney snatched her phone and answered.

"Hi there, lovely," he greeted. "We are on the way."

Layla's voice carried over the speaker. "Good. I'm glad. Is Heidi driving?"

"Yes, she is."

"Good."

Delaney fumbled. "W-what? I'm not that slow of a driver."

"Oh love..." Layla's voice held sympathy. "Yes, you are. Don't worry, I think it's adorable, but for now speed is best. Be careful now."

"We will."

"And Delaney?" she asked.

"Yes?"

"I love you and your slow driving. Mwah." She air-kissed through the phone and hung up.

"Cute," Heidi teased him.

"Don't even start, Rustler. I hear you say sweet nothings to Riley all the time."

"You bet I do. That man is for keeps." She wriggled the giant engagement ring that glistened on her finger. "You should get Layla one of these. I bet she'd say yes."

Delaney shifted uncomfortably in his seat. He always hated talking about his personal life, and Heidi loved to make him do so. "And who's to say I haven't?"

"Have you?" Heidi looked at him in surprise.

Delaney shrugged. "Perhaps."

"You haven't," Heidi stated. "You're just pulling my leg."

Delaney reached into his trouser pocket and withdrew a small box. Heidi gawked. "No way!"

He flicked it open and a beautiful solitaire stared up at her. "Delaney!" She punched him in the shoulder and a smile finally slipped through.

"Don't tell her," he ordered.

Heidi made a motion of zipping her lips. "How long have you had that?"

"A couple of months."

"Months?! And you haven't asked her?"

"Each time I think to, something comes about. I'd planned to the week I bought the ring but then Riley proposed to you and I didn't want to infringe upon that. I wished to this week and have had it in my pocket waiting until I saw her next, but it would seem I will need to wait a bit longer."

"No, you don't."

"Of course I do. I do not want to rob Rhea and Claron of their celebratory moment."

"And what would happen if you and I had a car accident right now and you never had the chance to ask her?"

"Don't be morbid, Heidi."

"Think about it and you know you would regret it. You need to ask her. And soon. If you love her that much, you'll want that ring on her finger as soon as possible."

Delaney and Layla

He felt like kissing the sidewalk when they arrived at the hospital, but he gladly opted for Layla's lips as she rushed towards him. "No baby yet, but they've admitted her. Aine says it is only a matter of time. Been laboring for over an hour already."

Heidi tossed Delaney her keys. "Just in case you wish to leave at some point. I'll be riding with Riley from here on out."

"Alright. And where shall I take your vehicle?"

Heidi shrugged. "Wherever. I know where you work." She grinned as Layla hustled them into an elevator. Delaney slipped the keys into his pocket, but the ring box was in the way, so he slipped them out to move to the other side. When he did, the small black box tumbled to the floor. The women looked down and Heidi's eyes widened. Layla turned to him, her eyes taking in his embarrassed face as he bent to retrieve the box.

"What is that?" she asked.

"'Tis... nothing. I've a pill box, is all. For my headaches." His words nervously tumbled over one another and Heidi smothered a laugh as Layla looked to her friend's amused gaze and then back to a pale Delaney. He swallowed the lump in his throat as she studied him.

"Are we to move?" Heidi asked, motioning towards the numbered buttons.

Layla opened her mouth to speak and then paused. "You don't take pills," she pointed out. "And I know what a bloody jewelry box looks like, Delaney. I'm not a fool."

"No, you're not." He ran a hand through his hair unsure of how to proceed.

"Well?" Layla asked.

"Well, what?" Delaney countered.

"Are you going to ask me or not?"

Delaney shook his head. "No. I'm not. Not here in... an elevator."

"Why not?" Layla asked. "It's as good a place as any."

"Because you deserve better than that. You deserve better than even knowing about it. I wished to surprise you with a romantic dinner, or a boat ride, or something other than a stuffy hospital elevator," Delaney explained.

Layla's face softened as she wrapped her arms around his neck and kissed him.

Heidi tried to slink to the farthest corner of the small elevator so as to not intrude on what was about to take place.

The elevator was most definitely stuffy as the doors had already closed. Layla had yet to tell them what floor Rhea was on and so they sat.

"Open the box, Delaney," Layla whispered.

Delaney studied her eyes a moment and then flicked open the little black box. Layla's eyes widened in surprise.

"Aren't you glad it wasn't earrings?" Heidi muttered.

Layla burst into a laugh as Delaney smirked at their friend.

"Layla," Delaney's voice quieted them all as he knelt to his knee. "I—"

The doors whooshed open and had them all turning to see a stunned Chloe and Conor as they waited to enter the elevator. Conor's face split into an earsplitting smile. "Well, what do we have here?"

"Bloody blast," Delaney mumbled as he ran an embarrassed hand over his face.

"A moment." Layla held up her hand to her sister and her beau. "Ask me, Delaney."

Clearing his throat and blocking out the surrounding people, he found her calm, hopeful blue eyes. "I love you, Layla," he began and saw her eyes glisten. "You've been so good for me. And to me, for that matter. Patient and kind and just enough demanding to bring me out of my shell."

Layla swiped a tear out of her eye and so did Chloe as she watched.

"I wished for a different moment, but as Heidi pointed out to me earlier, there is no time like the present. I love you and I wish to marry you, if you will have me. Will you marry me?"

Layla nodded and the others clapped and cheered as Delaney slipped the ring onto her finger and Layla kissed him. "I didn't bloody care where you asked me, Mr. Hawkins. I'm just glad you did." She kissed him once more before showing her new bauble to her sister and Heidi. Conor slapped him on the back and congratulated him.

"We don't wish to upstage Clary and Rhea," Layla told them. "So best keep this under wraps for today."

"Agreed." Delaney nodded as did the others. "That's what I was hoping to avoid as well."

"We can celebrate later," Layla assured him and then gave him a steamy kiss that left him fuzzy brained and everyone else in the elevator ready to step out. She reached over and pressed the button to the fifth floor. "We have a babe to meet."

∞

Layla poked her head into the room and a sweaty and tired Rhea glanced over. Claron sat next to her bed and held her hand and the nurses were scrolling something on their clipboards. Rhea smiled and motioned her inside. Heidi bolted past her and into the room. She reached Rhea in two strides and gripped her free hand. "How's it coming?"

"Slow," Claron reported, his gaze weary for his wife. Layla brushed a hand over Rhea's hair as Chloe walked in carrying a flower bouquet. She set it on the windowsill and rested a hand on her brother's shoulder as they all hovered around Rhea. "Is Riley still here?" she asked.

"Aye. He's busy bossing around Aine's nursing friends demanding more ice chips," Chloe reported. "He's roped Conor in on the hunt."

"Those boys are going to be the death of these poor nurses." Rhea smiled lovingly. "Anyone else arrived yet?"

"Mam and Da are on their way. They made a pit stop to pick up Roland and Evie."

"Declan will be here after his shift," Layla said. "Jaron and Jace when they're free from work. Murphy—" She slapped a hand to her forehead.

"I forgot Murphy and Piper!"

"No worries," Chloe told her. "I've spread the word to them. They were going to shut the pub down and be on their way."

"Oh, good. We're all here for you, Rhea love." Layla kissed her friend's hair. "And you, brother." She smiled at Claron and gripped his hand. "Exciting times."

Claron looked down at the hand he held and turned it over. "What's this?" His brow rose and showed it to Rhea.

Rhea's smile widened. "Looks like you have your own news."

"It can wait," Layla assured them. "But also exciting news. Now, hurry. Have this babe, Rhea. What do we need to do?"

"You need to step out of the room." A nurse walked into the room and towards Rhea. "I need to examine our mother-to-be." Layla squeezed her hand as Chloe straightened her blanket.

"Best of luck, Rhea darling." Layla tugged Heidi along with her as the women left.

Delaney awaited her in the waiting room along with a grumpy Riley and an amused Conor.

"I think we should move Rhea to a different hospital," Riley barked. "They aren't attentive enough."

"They're fine, brother." Chloe patted him on the back. "She's doing wonderfully. And there be no moving her now."

"I've found not one nurse who cares that she is out of ice," he grumbled, his hands on his hips. Heidi slipped her arms around him.

"Calm down, cowboy. She's in good hands."

Riley looked down at her and quickly gave her a peck on the lips. "'Tis hard, standing out here while she's in there suffering."

Layla burst into laughter. "I live to see the day Heidi is on the other side of that door and how you'll react when she's out of ice."

"He'll be my hero, I'm sure of it." Heidi grinned up at him and his face finally relaxed into a smile as he brushed a hand down her hair. "I'll be terrified," he admitted.

"Won't we all," Conor agreed. "Can't imagine the stress Clary feels, his lass all laid up and in pain."

"Oh come on," Chloe chuckled. "You lads act like we women are delicate creatures. Our bodies are made to bring babes into the world and there be no stronger person than our Rhea. I've no doubt she makes it look easy for us. Now, let's find us a seat and ready ourselves for Mam's arrival."

Layla sat next to Delaney and rested her chin on his shoulder as she stared at his handsome profile. Feeling her stare, he turned just enough for her to kiss his lips. He tucked a strand of hair behind her ear before brushing his finger down her cheek. "I love you, Mr. Hawkins," she whispered, and then rested her head against his shoulder and waited for more family to arrive.

Conor and Chloe

He'd grown to love the O'Rifcan family over the years and sitting in the cramped waiting room in the maternity ward of the hospital made him love them even more as they awaited the birth of Claron's baby. Conor heard the rest of them before he saw them. The remaining brothers. Lorena and her husband, Paul. Sidna and Senior. Roland and Evie. And bringing up the rear was Murphy and Piper. Senior's booming voice echoed down the halls as Aine led them towards the rest of the O'Rifcan bunch.

"Well?" Senior asked. "Do we have a babe?"

Chloe shook her head. "Been at it for hours, but no babe yet."

"Bless her." Sidna tsked her tongue. "Has she any chips?"

Riley waved a hand at his mother's concern as if finally an ally had been found.

Chloe grinned. "Aye. She has plenty of ice."

"I wonder if they'd let me in to see them." Sidna turned towards the door and walked over. She grabbed the first available nurse and asked. Waving Senior towards her, she motioned towards the door. "Roland, aren't you coming?" she clucked.

Roland walked forward as well as a nurse gave them the rules. She opened the door and they disappeared into the room.

"Is it weird that I feel better now that Mam is here?" Riley asked.

Layla laughed. "A mammy's boy, are you?"

"Maybe so."

"I think we all are," Jaron admitted. "I feel the same relief."

"Rhea's in good hands." Chloe gripped Conor's hand as if she wasn't sure of her own words and he patted the top of it.

"All is fine," he whispered to her.

"Should it be taking this long?" Chloe whispered. "It's been hours."

"It sometimes takes a while," Aine explained. "This isn't abnormal." She patted the bottom of her and Declan's newest addition and handed the little girl over to her father. The infant looked tiny in his large hands, but he expertly rested her in the crook of his arm.

Conor kissed Chloe's hand and her green eyes found his. "You think we'll be here one day?" she asked quietly.

"I hope so." He winked at her and she flushed.

"We haven't really talked of it." She said. "Perhaps we should. Not now," she amended. "But soon, perhaps."

"I'm already way ahead of you, lass." Conor winked at her and her lips spread into the sweet smile he'd grown to love more and more each day.

The door to Rhea's room burst open and Sidna barged through yelling for a doctor. "'Tis time!" she yelled. "'Tis time!"

The nurses rushed into the room to confirm Sidna's diagnosis and Senior and Roland were ushered into the hallway, the door closing behind them. A few minutes later the doctor hurried into the room.

Conor held Chloe next to his side as they all stood and waited expectantly.

∞

Chloe's heart sored when Claron stepped out of the room with two small babes wrapped in blankets. Her mother burst into tears at the sight as everyone stepped forward to gaze upon the tiny faces peeking out. One blue blanket, one pink.

"You rascal." Riley wriggled a hand through Claron's hair and beamed over his shoulder as he looked down at his newest niece and nephew. "They're beautiful."

Chloe lightly ran a finger over the little boy's cheek as Claron reported Rhea's recovery.

"Two?" Murphy shook his head in wonder as he elbowed his way forward to look upon the wee babes. "And they already have hats."

Chloe grinned up at her brother. "To keep them warm."

"What color hair do they have, Clary?" Murphy asked. "Can you tell?"

"Of course I can tell." Claron grinned as he removed the small pink hat from his little girl and black downy hair covered her head. The women squealed in pleasure at the sight and Murphy softly ran his hand over the small head. "Like fresh cotton."

"And the boyo?" Senior asked, just as mesmerized.

Claron removed the boy's hat and his hair was lighter than his sister's, his coloring more similar to Claron than to Rhea.

"One of each," Jace grinned. "Well done, brother."

"I'm to take them back now. Nurse said Rhea needs to tend to them for a bit. Visitors can come into the room in about a half hour." He looked up and his eyes bounced from one familiar face to the next. "Thank you all for being here."

"We wouldn't miss it," Chloe assured him and handed the pink hat back to him. "Go, take care of our Rhea. We'll shower you with love again in a bit."

"Thanks, sister." He kissed her cheek as he quietly made his way back into the room.

Layla sighed. "Have you ever seen such a tiny babe?"

Declan pointed to the one in his arms.

"Ah, true enough," Layla said. "Hard to believe we were all here just a couple of months ago for Aine and your wee one." She kissed the little girl's cheek. "She already seems so big."

"It goes by fast," Aine admitted.

"I want a dozen," Heidi said, staring longingly at the door.

Riley laughed. "Easy now, love. One step at a time."

"A dozen was my hope as well," Sidna stated. "I settled for ten." She chuckled. "And I couldn't be happier with the lot of ye."

Tommy kissed his mother's cheek as she reached for Declan's little girl and bounced her in her arms. "The more children, the more grandchildren." Her eyes sparkled as she set about her grandmotherly task of rocking a baby to sleep.

Chloe reached for Conor's hand as they walked back to their seats, grateful for a man that understood the importance of family and sat amongst them with no complaint. She felt a tug on her hand and noticed Conor slipping a ring onto her finger. She stifled her gasp as he held a finger to his lips with a small smirk. She looked down at the antique ring and knew immediately that he'd given her a family heirloom. She hopped to her feet, the rest of her family eyeing her with curiosity. "Conor and I will be right back." She pulled him to his feet and down the hall. She found the first vacant room and jumped into his arms. His hearty laugh seeped through her heart and to her toes as he wrapped his strong arms around her.

"Am I a fool to ask you now?"

"Not a'tall, Conor McCarthy. 'Tis the perfect time."

"Good. I've wanted this for a long while, Chloe love. A long while. Will you be my wife?"

"Aye. Most definitely." Beaming, she giggled as a nurse stumbled upon them and frowned. She wriggled her ring finger at the woman and the nurse nodded in understanding before going on her way.

Murphy and Piper

"We have company," Claron announced as he walked into the living room followed by Murphy and Piper. Rhea looked up expectantly as she held her son in her arms.

"Good to see you home, Rhea." Piper sat down next to her and accepted the small babe in glee. She beamed up at Murphy as she settled against the cushions.

"She's been wanting to hold those babes since the hospital." Murphy grinned as he looked in wonder at the little girl in Claron's arms.

"How's the new mam and da doing?" Piper asked.

"Tired," they replied in unison and then smiled at one another.

"I bet. How's that 3 AM milking going these days, Clary?" Murphy hooted in laughter as little green eyes stared up at him. "I say..." He leaned down and studied the girl's face. "She's to have eyes like you soon, Clary. Looks like."

"Aye. We think so too." Claron beamed proudly as he offered his daughter towards Murphy. His brother took a cautious step back.

"You don't want to hold her?" Rhea asked.

"Best not. I've never held a babe."

"Not even Lorena's or Aine's?"

"No," Murphy answered.

"Come now, Murphy. She doesn't bite. Yet." Claron chuckled as he eased the babe into his brother's arms. She squirmed a bit and Murphy snuggled her close so as not to drop her. Piper watched as his face softened and he lightly kissed the girl's dark hair. "How do you sleep at night, brother?"

Claron's brow furrowed. "What do you mean?"

"I think I'd stare at them all night long," Murphy admitted.

"We do," Rhea replied. "It's hard not to. They're so beautiful and small."

Murphy walked towards Rhea and gently leaned down and kissed her forehead. "You did a brilliant job, Rhea love. Absolutely brilliant."

"Hey now, I contributed," Claron told him.

"Contributed." Murphy scoffed and had the women laughing. "We all know who did the real work." He winked at Rhea.

"Sorry we had to run out on the celebration, but me da was having his ceremony," Piper explained.

"Don't apologize. Six months sober is worth celebrating," Rhea acknowledged.

"He definitely had his setbacks in the beginning," Piper shared. "But he's never made it to a milestone. Gives me hope that Da will continue on this path. Murphy's been a wonder with him."

Murphy waved away her praise. "Daniel's a good man. He's got his head on straight now. A real help around the pub."

"I'm so glad." Rhea patted Piper's thigh as Piper cued over the baby.

"We missed the big announcement," Murphy said. "What did you name them?"

A knock sounded on the door and Riley poked his head inside carrying various balloons. "Hello to the house!" he called, making sure all the balloons made it safely through the doorway before closing the door.

"And what have we here?" Claron asked. "You've already showered us with gifts, brother."

Riley grinned. "I've come to see my little mini me." He beamed down at the little girl in Murphy's arms. "Looking more and more like me every day." He kissed Rhea and Piper on the cheeks as he nestled the balloons in the corner of the room by the baby swings.

"We were just about to tell Murphy and Piper their names," Rhea told him.

"They don't know yet? Oh, right. They had to leave early. You're going to love them," Riley beamed.

Laughing, Claron looked to Rhea. "I told you we should have named her something different."

Rhea smiled tenderly at Riley and rolled her eyes. "Don't make me regret it."

He held up his hand as he waved her onward.

"Our little girl is Fíona Riley," Rhea announced.

Murphy shook his head as Riley did a small jig. "I've a namesake!"

"And that be Sydney Niall," Claron motioned towards his son in Piper's arms.

Murphy's eyes widened. "Niall?"

"Aye. After you, brother."

Piper watched as sheer joy washed over Murphy's face. "Me?"

"Our hope is that one day our little ones will be as kind as their uncles. And show that kindness to others just as you did to their mother." Rhea leaned over Piper and brushed her hand over her son's head.

"Rhea darling, I'm speechless." Murphy held a hand over his heart.

"That's a first," Piper added, making them all laugh.

"Hey now, love. We've yet to tell them our good news, haven't we?"

"News?" Rhea asked.

"Aye." Murphy ignored Piper's pleading glance. "Piper doesn't wish to share it because we're here to see the new babes."

Rhea looked quickly to Piper's ring finger and noticing it bare, looked confused. Piper chuckled.

"It's not that," she stated.

"Piper's moved to Castlebrook," Murphy announced. "Permanently."

"I thought she already had?" Claron looked even more confused than Rhea.

"Aye. Sort of," Murphy explained.

"What he means is, I've moved in with him."

Surprise registered on Rhea and Claron's faces. "Oh."

"As my wife," Murphy continued.

Claron turned to his brother in shock. Piper felt they should have waited before telling anyone, but as Claron hugged his brother tightly and Riley practically lifted him off his feet, mindful of the baby, she felt herself smiling.

"Her ring is currently being resized," Murphy told Rhea.

"When did this happen?"

"Yesterday," Murphy reported. "We didn't make a fuss because well, we didn't want one. We wished to tie the knot on our own. Evelyn and Daniel were our witnesses, as well as Mam and Da. All very private," Murphy continued.

Blinking back her bafflement, Rhea reached for Piper again. "Wow, I'm so happy for you guys."

"Thanks." Piper blushed and looked down at Sydney's sweet face.

"Piper played hard to get, but in the end she couldn't say no." Murphy winked at his new bride and she rolled her eyes.

"I've no idea why I said yes."

Murphy stuck his tongue out at Piper and Rhea laughed. "I think it's absolutely wonderful and worth celebrating. We should call everyone to come over for a meal."

Claron's brows lifted.

"How about," Riley began, "we save celebrating for another day, Rhea darling, so that you and Clary can get some much needed rest while we offer to hold and sit with the little ones?"

"That sounds like my kind of party," Claron admitted.

Rhea looked tempted.

"Go," Piper told her. "We'll watch them. You two need a nap."

"I think I've fallen more in love with all of you." Rhea reached for Claron's hand and they headed up the new staircase to their finished master suite.

∞

"Nice of you to offer watching the babes, brother," Murphy told Riley as he switched babies with Piper. He now held Sydney and enjoyed learning everything about the wee lad as he studied his tiny fingers.

"I'm not watching them. You two are." Riley grinned as he walked towards the door. "I'm to meet Heidi."

"You sneak." Murphy slapped him on the back as he departed. "He's always been good at that."

Piper chuckled as Murphy eased onto the sofa next to her. They each held the tiny humans in their laps facing towards them.

"They've different shapes to their noses. See that?" Murphy pointed out.

"A wee bit, yeah. Fíona has a rounder face than Sydney," Piper observed.

"I think Fíona has the bigger appetite by the looks of it. Isn't that right, lass?"

He grunted as Piper elbowed him in the side on a laugh. "She's perfect."

"Aye. She is. They both are." He leaned towards Piper and kissed her temple. "Thanks for marrying me, Piper love. I sit here in wonder over these babes and can't help but think our time will come one day."

"It will."

"Yeah?"

"Of course," Piper told him. "How could we deprive the world of another Murphy O'Rifcan?"

His hearty laugh had Fíona scrunching up her face. "Oh no, now you've done it." He began shushing the baby as he gently bounced her in his hands. "'Tis not *that* bad of an idea, Fíona. Calm down now. 'Twill be for a while yet. Don't be upset by feeling upstaged."

Piper elbowed him again and he grinned. "Whenever the time comes, Murphy, I look forward to it with you."

"Aye. Me too, lass. Me too." And the kiss they shared over the tiny onlookers sealed more than just the promise of cherished memories, but the promise of a blossoming future.

Chicago's Best

https://www.amazon.com/dp/B06XH7Y3MF

Montgomery House

https://www.amazon.com/dp/B073T1SVCN

Beautiful Fury

https://www.amazon.com/dp/B07B527N57

All titles by Katharine E. Hamilton Available on Amazon and Amazon Kindle

Adult Fiction:

The Unfading Lands Series
The Unfading Lands, Part One
Darkness Divided, Part Two
Redemption Rising, Part Three

The Lighthearted Collection
Chicago's Best
Montgomery House
Beautiful Fury

The Siblings O'Rifcan Series
Claron
Riley
Layla
Chloe
Murphy

Children's Literature:
The Adventurous Life of Laura Bell
Susie At Your Service
Sissy and Kat

Short Stories:
If the Shoe Fits

Find out more about Katharine and her works at:
www.katharinehamilton.com

Social Media is a great way to connect with Katharine. Check her out on the following:

Facebook: Katharine E. Hamilton
https://www.facebook.com/Katharine-E-Hamilton-282475125097433/

Twitter: @AuthorKatharine
Instagram: @AuthorKatharine

Contact Katharine:
khamiltonauthor@gmail.com

ABOUT THE AUTHOR

Katharine E. Hamilton began writing a decade ago by introducing children to three fun stories based on family and friends in her own life. Though she enjoyed writing for children, Katharine moved into adult fiction in 2015 with the release of her first novel, The Unfading Lands, a clean, epic fantasy that landed in Amazon's Hot 100 New Releases on its fourth day of publication and reached #72 in the Top 100 Bestsellers on all of Amazon in its first week. The series did not stop there and the following two books in The Unfading Lands series released in late 2015 and early 2016.

Though comfortable in the fantasy genre, Katharine decided to venture into romance in 2017 and released the first novel in a collection of sweet, clean romances: The Lighthearted Collection. The collection's works would go on to reach bestseller statuses and win Reader's Choice Awards and various Indie Book Awards in 2017 and early 2018.

Katharine has contributed to charitable Indie anthologies and helped other aspiring writers journey their way through the publication process. She loves everything to do with writing and loves that she can continue to share heartwarming stories to a wide array of readers.

She was born and raised in the state of Texas, where she currently resides on a ranch in the heart of brush country with her husband, Brad, and their son, Everett, and their two furry friends, Tulip and Cash. She is a graduate of Texas A&M University, where she received a bachelor's degree in History.

She is thankful to her readers for allowing her the privilege to turn her dreams into a new adventure for us all.

CPSIA information can be obtained
at www.ICGtesting.com
Printed in the USA
LVHW110048130722
723380LV00024B/233

9 780578 484587